Lock Down Publications and Ca$h
Presents

THE PLUG'S RUTHLESS DAUGHTER 2

BLACK CARTEL GIRL

Tony Daniels

Lock Down Publications
P.O. Box 944
Stockbridge, GA 30281
www.lockdownpublications.com

Like our page on Facebook: Lock Down Publications
www.facebook.com/lockdownpublications.ldp

Stay Connected with Us!

Text **LOCKDOWN** to 22828 to stay up-to-date with new releases, sneak peaks, contests and more…

Like our page on Facebook:
Lock Down Publications

Join Lock Down Publications/The New Era Reading Group

Visit our website:
www.lockdownpublications.com

Follow us on Instagram:
Lock Down Publications

Email Us: We want to hear from you!

Acknowledgements

First and foremost, I want to give all praise and thanks to Allah. I want to thank my kids for their undying support and genuine love during these tumultuous times and struggles.

Shoutout to all the solid stand-up good men and women incarcerated in every federal prison. A special shoutout to Ms. Mills because she put up with so much shit and kept it real. You have taught me how to deal with different issues in life. Thank you.

Now, shoutout to the stand-up niggas from the "Blind Justice" indictment that kept it real in 2015 and the ones didn't you know who you are. The ones I missed—much respect and love . . . catch you next time.

Hard work pays off to success!

Dedication

To my son Tardius Daniels that I love and missed so much. Always remember that you will be missed and loved forever.

Love—Your Daddy

Rewind

Jazz took a deep breath and started talking, telling Mustafa everything she knew about the other guys, where they hung out, where they stayed, and what they did. It took her twenty-five minutes to explain to him as they rode around.

Mustafa knew he couldn't send her home; that would be going into a death trap, so he took her to a hotel room to chill out while he went to holla at Boss Lady and drop off the duffle bags to her.

***

Boss Lady didn't have time to waste. She wheeled her carry-on luggage behind the stream of people, looking stunning in a figure-flattering white t-shirt that revealed ample cleavage. The loud noise was giving her a damn headache, especially the suited Asian man talking in a loud pitch on his phone. She hissed. She felt like striking him upside his damn head just because of the racket he was making. She pulled out her cell phone and dialed Mustafa's phone number, walking briskly toward the terminal exit as she heard the phone ringing. It was a warm, cloudless morning. She stepped outside into the hot sun, her eyebrows knitted tight in anger. "Pick up, nigga, bitch ass nigga," she said to herself, her heels click-clacking against the gleaming flooring.

"Yeah."

"Mustafa, I'm here. I need your location because I'm about to jump into a cab and head your direction."

"We're at Holiday Inn off the Main Turnpike, room 404."

"Holiday Inn?" She was taken aback. She figured she would be given a lavish overtop address, but temporary because of the murders.

"Yeah, that's correct."

"Okay, I'll be there once I get into a local cab. And keep your head up, Mustafa. I'm here now, nigga." She laughed. A lot had to be done, and she was determined to get it done. But the question was, how? Now that so many different Cartels had moved into the city, there would be more drug wars. This wasn't her city, but she brought with her that Memphis attitude and her wicked street smarts. And, together, she and Mustafa were going to continue to get money. *To be honest, we don't give a damn about the Daniels Cartel at all*, she thought.

She threw her luggage into the trunk and climbed into the backseat in one of several cabs idling outside the terminal. She told the female driver her destination. The driver nodded and maneuvered her way out the airport and toward the freeway. The weather was too hot, so Boss Lady rolled down the window to let a cool breeze waft into the cab. "How long before I reach my location?" she asked the cab driver.

"About thirty-five-minutes," the local cab driver said.

Boss Lady sighed and leaned into the seat. She checked her cell phone for messages, but there were none. She could hear the engine roaring underneath the small hood. The driver had a lead foot, and she was pleased. She was swerving in and out of lanes, hitting speeds up to 80 mph in the sparse early morning traffic.

The cab driver pulled into the curved entryway in the front of the Holiday Inn. The place was a stone entryway in the front of the hotel. It was a stone's throw from the freeway. She paid the cab driver her fee, and she removed her bag from the trunk. She stared at the seven-story structure, the hotel's logo perched on top, the exterior hallway and long white railings on each floor. She made her way inside. The lobby was quiet and quaint, no marble flooring, or extravagant structures like towering waterfalls and stoned statues. There was complimentary fresh brewed coffee in the lobby. She strolled past the clerk behind a stretched reception desk cluttered with pamphlets and various things. The clerk raised her head from the computer screen, noticed the luggage she was wheeling, and didn't attempt to say anything or ask questions. She went on with her business.

Boss Lady pushed for the small elevator and waited. It didn't take as long as she thought. She stepped out and searched for room 404. It was the last door down the long hallway. To her left were the teal room doors, and to her right, a three-story drop over the railing, and beyond that, a bland gas station next door, a few local bullshitting businesses across the street, and farther down the street, sprawling nice homes that stretched for many miles.

The door to the room opened and she stood face to face with Mustafa. She already saw the wear and tear happening with him. His hair was in disarray. "You look like shit," she said. Before she could walk inside well enough, Mustafa collapsed into her arms and started crying like a baby. She clutched him tight and embraced her lovingly. "I'm here, sweetie. I'm here to help out wit' this," she said.

"Baby, we must relocate somewhere else because this shit crazy outta here."

She continued to hold Mustafa in her arms, consoling him. She surveyed the room, and spotted four handguns on the wooden round long table along with food. The shades were closed and the room reeked of weed. The television was on, showing small clips on the news but it was on mute.

Ironically, the screen was displaying Boss Lady's and Mustafa's recent work, the bodies found over a period of time in the hood. Neither one of them really watched the local news, and they wanted to forget about it at the moment. She took a seat on the bed. She had to be the strong person in this situation, even though the news shit hit her hard, reminding her of the past crimes she committed.

Jazz started telling them about the high ransom murderers and kidnappers were asking for, and even mentioned Mustafa's name. She had an inside plug to resolve this matter for a small fee, but she hadn't mentioned it yet to them. "To be honest, the detectives don't have anything. They can't charge you for making hits on people or prove that several phone calls led to many deaths," Jazz said.

He kissed Boss Lady on the forehead and started thinking about all the shit they sold to pay bills. Her bank account was now damn near empty to the point she was thinking about getting government help for housing and food. The things that Jazz said may be true or false, but on the other end it was better to play the safe side. If Ebony was talking or bragged about being a killer, that was it. The worst thing that could occur would be Jazz getting that information, responding and using it against them. He could not believe she would snitch. But if he did, she would turn it back around on him and say they lied on her. Ebony was a cold bitch. The government was playing the system, and the justice system was letting them do it. Technically, the cops didn't have any evidence, circumstantial or otherwise. They used the theory, *let's arrest her and let the pieces of the puzzle fall in place.* And they knew the weakest link always spilled the brown beans. It was a gamble, but they had several murder cases to close. And they didn't want it to end up in the cold file.

In the heart of the city where the shadows tainted up more secrets than the stars above, Ebony paced the worn floorboards of an old mill next to the Holiday Inn that served as the cartel's hideout. She went for a walk to ease her mind without saying anything. The scent of stale cigarettes mingled with the faint fragrance of gunpowder in the air. The perfume of the illicit trade that had defined her life for so long. She had long been a fixture in the underworld. All knew her as the vice grip of the cartel, unyielding, fierce, and devoted to the cause. She went back into the hotel, and things didn't feel right. Her phone vibrated, the call flashing an unknown number, but she didn't need to see the name to know it was the feds. They'd been onto her, giving her the option to turn federal witness, to betray the trust of those she'd come to see as family. In return, they waved the carrot of her freedom, a life in the sun, away from the long shadow of the drug ring. Ebony was immovable as stone. Her mind had been made up long before the call had ever come. She knew the cost of her decisions, the weight of the chain she'd put around her neck with every shipment, every maneuver to expand their territory. And she'd quieted her conscience with the belief that if it ever came crashing down, she'd take the fall alone.

The cartel was more than crime, it was a surrogate family born from necessity, from survival. Each member carried their scars, their stories, their reasons for staying, and she was inked deep into her very core. Jazz stayed in the bathroom for a minute and seemed like she was on the phone talking.

The sound of sirens soon echoed in the distance, cutting through the thick silence. It was time. With a reinforced resolve, Ebony decided her path. She would be the scapegoat, the singular figure to serve as the dam against the deluge. By her silence, the other might continue, might live out what lives could be salvaged in the aftermath. She penned a letter, a final testament to be delivered to the only person left that mattered to her, Mustafa. In it she laid out her heart, the whys and the because, the understanding she sought and the forgiveness she hoped would one day come. She kissed him on the lips and tears rolled down both of their faces. Turning from the past, she stepped out into the open, beneath the blinking stars, and walked towards the nearing lights of police cars. She surrendered without a fight, was read her rights, and taken into custody. She confronted the glaring lights of interrogation, the pressing gaze of the officers, and the probing questions that sought to unravel the web of the cartel. But she offered name, rank, and serial number. Beyond that, she remained an enigma, her words sealing shut, a tomb that refused to release the dead.

***

Ebony's trial was a media circus, the public ravenous for details of the drug ring that had pumped venom into the city's veins. But no matter the heat of the prosecution's grilling, no matter their promises or threats, she remained stoic, her lips pressed into a line of defiance. In her silence, the trial reached its inevitable conclusion. A guilty verdict on multiple counts, the full penalty laid heavy on her sole shoulders.

She entered the federal prison with the same quiet fortitude that had earned her the respect of everyone, from foot soldiers to kingpin. The prison was a different beast, its walls lined with the burdened souls of countless stories, but she adapted with a fluid grace that spoke of an inner strength. Her reputation preceded her, a tale whispered across the meager freedoms of the yard: that of a woman who bore her punishment as a badge of loyalty, an honor by betrayal.

Years ticked by, scribing their passage across her skin in the form of aging that even the stone-cold silence of the pen couldn't keep at bay. She received no visits from her former associates, a bitter favor as they stayed shadowed, alive. But there were letters from Mustafa, each a balm to his chaffed spirit, each a glimpse into the world she'd left behind.

Finally, as seasons cycled and the calendar marked time's inexorable march, Jazz's sentence drew to an end. She'd served her sentence with her head high, a reed strong enough to bend but never break. Upon her release, she soaked in the sun's rays, a stark contrast to the cold artificial light she'd grown accustomed to. She was free, not just from jail, but from the chains of her past life. The burden of the cartel had been lifted, leaving behind only the weight of time lost.

Ebony joined Mustafa, who had flourished in her absence, her path untarnished by the darkness that had once threatened to engulf them both. Together, they embraced, two survivors of a storm that had taken so much yet given them this moment of rebirth, but broke at the same time.

In a quiet nook in the world, away from the crime and the clamor of an old identity, Ebony found room for forgiveness, first for herself and then, from those she loved. Silence had been her choice, her unwavering stance, and now in the twilight of her ordeal, she discovered a new voice, one that didn't speak of drugs or power or defiance, but of hope, of change, and of the strength to be unbreakable loyal, even if it meant facing the darkness alone. She had transcended her own legend, the cartel woman who chose jail over betrayal. Her story was finished, but her life's quiet new chapter was just beginning.

Chapter 1

Junebug was standing on the street corner, selling crack to the fiends in the hood. He started selling crack at the age of fifteen in the neighborhood on the eastside of town. His homie—Ace—fronted him twenty rocks at a time, and he made five dollars' profit from each rock he sold to keep money in his pocket for hard times. At the age of twenty, he was buying six ounces of powder cocaine. After a couple months later, he had his own trap spot and purchased his first car for $800.00 a black 1988 Monte Carlo with glass T-Tops. His brother and sister held a special place in his heart.

Peanut was a straight-up killer as well a true player around the block, but he enjoyed buying sex from junkies in the hood and getting his dick sucked by different bitches that he thought was beautiful but was on some kind of drugs to fuck with the mind. He loved to fuck crackheads that he thought will change their life one day and become a star from the hood and be with him forever. He was a tall slim cat and weighed around 185 pounds of muscle, with a mouth full of diamond teeth. He turned the streets of a small town into a battle zone. To be honest, his friend—Tip—didn't know he'd been fucking with his girlfriend, Mimi, for some time now.

"Ain't that a bitch!" Mimi said to herself while chilling at her crib, staring at the results from her pregnancy test. She was sitting around the crib in her bra and panties. Her boyfriend—Tip—took a trip to Memphis to handle some business. "Shit, I cannot believe a bitch is pregnant around this bitch. Tip gon' have to slow his ass down because I'm not raising my baby by myself around this bitch. Fuck that shit! He can have all this material shit and money." She was afraid that the feds might catch him or he would get killed in the streets from dealing drugs. "Either he gon' slow his ass down and leave these streets alone, or I'm getting an abortion. It's as simple as that!"

She was caught up in her thoughts. A loud knock at the front door caught her attention. She went to the door and creaked open the door, standing there half naked.

"Damn, this bitch pussy fat," Peanut said to himself, as his dick stood straight up in his Polo jeans.

"What's up, Peanut baby?"

"Not shit, trying to find Tip ass to handle some business. Looking at your fine ass got a nigga thinking something else right now."

She had a perky set of B cups with pinkish nipples, a toned stomach, thick thighs and a nice round ass like Megan Thee Stallion.

"What's the business, Peanut?"

"Is your nigga around here?" He laughed.

"Nawl, he gone somewhere to handle some business in another state right now. Are you going to stand here looking handsome, or you gonna come inside and let me do something strange to you real quick?" She turned around and bent over, pulling her panties to the side with her small hands, giving Peanut a clear view of her fat pussy that he had been beating up for a while on the low.

He walked inside of the house and locked the front door behind him like he lived there for many years. "Baby, a nigga really do care about you. My love is strong for you, as you can see."

"Baby, a bitch loves you too." She smiled at him.

"Damn, baby girl, I cannot believe you mentioned that to a local player like myself? Girl, I love you so much." Peanut pulled her body against his strong arms and kissed her wet strawberry lips.

She pushed Peanut down on the couch, pulled off his clothes, and straddled across his lap. She reached for his throbbing dick and directed it slowly inside of her creamy pussy. "Ummnn!" She moaned from the pleasure and pain she was feeling. Increasing her pace, she rode him like a cowgirl on a horse with no saddle. "Ohh, my god! Umn, I love you and this huge dick, Peanut!" The feeling of his 13 inches of hard steel was driving her insane. She grabbed the back of his bald head and guided his mouth to her right nipple. "Baby, suck here, I'm about to bust loose like a machine gun at war. Oh, shit! I'm cumin', nigga! Ahhnn!" She moaned as she released a truck load of cum all over his big dick.

With his huge hammer dick inside her pussy, he carried her over to the dining room. He slipped his big dick out of her wet pussy, as he let her down slowly. "Bend your thick ass over and put your head between your ankles like you Pinky the porn star." She did as he instructed her to. "Now, lean your back against the wall."

"Peanut, a bitch not a young thot anymore." She laughed. She got into her position, her pussy sprouted from between her thighs, and it was so wet that she could see her vaginal secretions dripping on the floor. He knelt down behind her and feasted on her asshole like a free buffet dinner. She gripped the back of his head like a baseball with her small hands. She was flexible as hell. "Nawl, nigga, eat this pussy some more," she said, as she directed his head back down between her legs. He was eating her pussy like it was his last meal on earth. He buried his long tongue deep inside her pussy, and skillfully dipped it in and out and down her slit. Simultaneously, he reached his hands around her thick legs and used his long middle finger to massage her clitoris. "Yes, daddy! Eat this pussy up," she said as he continued to fuck her with his long tongue, after finishing massaging her clitoris with his middle finger.

Peanut's head game was on a thousand, for sure. "Have you ever had some head like that?" After getting her pussy eaten, she craved the feeling of hardcore sex penetration into her stomach. "Fuck me harder, young nigga, this time!"

He stood to his feet, crouched on top of her, and buried his pipe deep inside her wet asshole. He slammed his thighs against her wet ass, working on a broken city road that needed to be fixed quickly, as his long strokes were making her cum instantly back-to-back from the hard pain she was taking from his dick.

"Ahhnn!" she screamed. "Fuck yeah, this your pussy, Peanut. You can fuck me some more in all my holes on my body." He beat her pussy up for about forty-five minutes with nice and strong strokes, and they came together and laid on the floor, holding each other's body.

One hour later, Peanut got up and put his clothes on. He grabbed Mimi's phone and entered a code number that would enable her to call him when she woke up. Peanut placed a soft kiss on her lips and said, "Baby, my number is in your phone. Call me when you get up." She couldn't believe that Peanut was leaving her with a wet ass from all the beating she took from his huge dick that got her stomach and body parts hurting. Peanut exited the front door without saying another word again. She was so upset that she got up and prepared herself to take a nice hot shower and laid back down to sleep.

Chapter 2

The next night was a nightmare when a disrespectful act caused the first of many murders. Ebony was one of the most beautiful women you have ever seen. Peanut considered her to be his queen for the rest of his life. Several crew members tried to rape her and molest her after a long night at Club Blue. She had several drinks that had her down for the count feeling good as hell. She was dancing across the floor and tossing that nice ass in a circle on anybody that she could get to dance with her. This caused a fury of hate to come about.

Moe was a large drug dealer around the hood, but didn't know that Ebony was Peanut's main thot. She was a ruthless bitch killer that would protect her man with her own life in the streets. She was crazy about Mustafa, but she let the feds come in between them and she had to relocate to get a new start. The feds had dropped all charges against her and changed her name to Ebony William. She had a strong vision of becoming a nurse or college teacher one day.

Now Peanut decided to make Moe feel the pain by killing everything he ever cherished in his whole life, including his family, pets, friends, and most of all his mother, whom he loved the most. Moe's main problem was that he never paid enough attention to his surroundings and his so-called friends. They didn't realize they were being watched by a cold killer that cared about nothing, even his own life, but would go as far as he had to conquer his mission set forward.

Inside of the stolen car the eyes of two masked men gazed upon three members of Junebug's drug organization, as they carried two black and red duffle bags into the house. The two men had been plotting on this for months now and were interested in getting their hands on what they knew was inside of those bags: cash or a large amount of street drugs. On any given day, thirty-six to a hundred kilos of cocaine made its way in and out the spot.

The two men sat silently for a moment, as they realized what they had to do next. They grabbed their loaded 9 millimeter handguns and took a few deep breaths, as they readied themselves to make a power move.

"You ready?" one of the dudes said.

"Hell yeah, I'm ready to handle business!"

The men burst out of the car fast as hell. They aimed their guns as they began to squeeze their triggers at the workers without a delay. All three men were caught off guard and became targets head-on. Within four minutes, the masked men had leveled the men to the ground, killing them with head and torso shots. The two men raced over to the bags and, without checking the contents, they knew they had come up.

Three men dead and over three hundred kilos of pure cocaine stolen from the organization. This was a first for the biggest hit they had ever taken. Not to know that many more cartels had been moving in slowly.

"We did," one of the guys said.

"I told you it was sweet as hell," Moe said, as he drove the red Range Rover down the block. "Fuck them bitch ass niggas. They shouldn't be getting all this money out here anyways, player . . . this our fuckin' hood. Plus, they work for Peanut and Junebug, you know how a nigga feel about other drug dealers. Fuck 'em," Moe said as he pulled off his mask.

"Moe," the other man said, "I'm just home from the feds from doing twenty years in Yazoo Mississippi prison . . . they treat you like shit, and especially the black officers. If I ain't eatin' then I'm killing anyone who stands in my way of me feeding my family. I'm about to be the man around here since others been long gone around this bitch."

Both men were geeked up as they looked into one of the duffle bags and saw the pure cocaine.

"We rich as shit!"

"Not yet, youngin'. We still got to get rid of this dope," Moe replied.

This score was going to be life-changing and they knew that they would have to protect themselves because once the word got out that it was them who'd done that shit, there would surely be a price tag on their heads. The crew were fully aware of the consequences before they'd executed the robbery, but the reward was worth the risk.

Moe was a short dude and had a short temper. Dark-skinned, he was a known street thug from Blytheville, Arkansas. He had spent half of his thirties in prison. He had murdered over twelve men, mostly drug dealers. Now, with the three he had just killed added to his list, he could care less if he had to kill some more. People in the streets knew him as a killer. He would be off with your head in a heartbeat. He had no conscience, and his only motivation was to get a quick score and to make his life easier. He wasn't about starting from the bottom; he wanted to get to the top real fast as possible. He ran a small circle and a hitman crew of known thieves called "Head Busters", and his young nephew—Fresh—would be a damn fool to give the same respect to someone else and not his uncle.

Although Moe wanted to help his nephew out there in the streets, there was no loyalty in him at all from past experience. Moe knew in his heart that war can break loose after this shit, and wanted to do whatever he had to get his man.

***

Tip made a turnaround back to the city to check on his girlfriend. He sat at the red light looking crazy in the face, as he took another look at the exquisite platinum and diamond ring that he picked up for his girlfriend. While he was on the road, he not only found the perfect land to buy for their dream home built on, but also the perfect engagement ring to ask her hand in marriage.

He couldn't wait to get home to the woman that he loved the most. He really couldn't wait to see the look on her face when he asked her to be his wife. He wanted it to be today, but all the drama caused him to pause for a moment, or two. He wanted it to be a moment they could both remember many years from now. He was going to wait until he came up with the perfect plan. Maybe it was just him, but today was the loveliest summer day ever for a handsome player. The weather wasn't too hot. The air smelled fresh and the birds seemed to be chirping in a harmonious melody. The only thing that worried him was the fact that he hadn't been able to reach her, since he had been in traffic. Every time he called her, the phone would go to voicemail. He made himself think she was probably in the shower or gone to the corner store to get something to eat. Being that his drug business had been taken care of sooner than expected, he decided to come back home because of the love he has for her. He couldn't stand the thought of being away from her for too long. He just didn't know somebody was getting that pussy.

As he headed to the crib, he tried to call her phone back several times, but there wasn't an answer at all. He tried calling Peanut and Junebug's phone, but nobody picked up the phone either. At this moment he was really thinking crazy shit through his mind. The last thing he wants to think was his bitch fucking another nigga.

***

Twenty minutes later, he arrived at his crib. The first thing he noticed when he walked into the house was: his future wife was sitting on the couch looking crazy in the face. She seemed relaxed and sipping on a glass of Moët to ease the mind and soul. She had the lights dimmed and the soulful music of her favorite singer—Adele—was grooving through the calm night air. He smiled as he watched his girlfriend sing along to the song with her eyes closed. She was in the groove, but once she felt a gaze upon her, she quickly opened her eyes and was startled.

"Baby, how long you been standing there?" He walked over to her and sat down beside her.

"For just a few minutes, but long enough to know that man really has you in a good mood right now." He was playing mind games on her. "He got that feel good music for you, huh?" he played more, causing her to laugh softly, as he pulled her closer into his strong arms.

"You know, she has a great voice," she said, kissing his forehead and lips.

"Yeah, real good answer. I know your birthday is around the corner. Maybe we could go to one of Adele's concerts in Memphis, TN . . . one day."

"Really, I would love that shit, baby."

"Good, well, enough of Adele. I think your man wants a piece of your pie right now," he said, laying her down on the couch for a nice surprise.

They exchanged a heated kiss before she interrupted him. "Maybe we should head upstairs, because my friend girl is in the other room."

"That's an excellent idea because once I get this dick inside of you, your lungs are going to have one hell of a workout tonight."

"Oh, really. Yeah, you know a bitch can't take too much dick in her stomach."

He slapped her on the ass cheeks, as they walked upstairs toward their bedroom. They entered the room, and he closed the door behind them.

"I hope that you're ready for this workout about to hit you, because you're gonna need all the energy you can get for this fuck session. You might need a COVID-19 mask too," he said, laughing.

She enjoyed the playful side of him. He was often serious with the amount of business and problems that were always weighing him down. Tonight she was ready for the softer, lighter side he displayed, but she also knew what was about to get laid down on her ass was going to be a serious problem to her pussy. He was no punk bitch when it came to maintaining her pussy. He was all man and some, in and out the bedroom. She succumbed to his every wish and demand, as he took charge and fulfilled her sexual desire and need.

He stuck his middle finger inside of her pussy and took it out and placed it inside her mouth. "Baby, this pussy is wet as hell like a water fountain flowing through the stream."

"Damn, my pussy tastes good." She unzipped his pants and took his large manhood out and placed it inside her wet mouth. She made sure she caught every drop of cum down her throat. The bitch was so bad she didn't let none hit the floor. "How many people you know can do that? This cum is the best I ever tasted in my whole life. You have anything I can wipe my mouth with? My pussy is wet as hell right now. Baby, a bitch needs you to beat this pussy up. I've been a bad little girl. I need you to handle this before I head back downstairs to check on my homegirl."

"Here, take this Polo shirt and clean your mouth." He laughed.

As she was wiping her mouth, he pulled out his dick again and bent her down on the bed with her face in the pillow. He placed his dick inside of her pussy from the back, causing her to let out a loud moan through the bedroom.

"Please don't hurt me. Please, baby. Give it to me, give it all to me. Please, baby."

"Damn, baby!" he shot back, hungrily biting down on his bottom lip. He closed his eyes appreciatively, savoring the feeling that ignited through the stroking of her wet walls which were contracting around his erection. "Damn, a real nigga love being inside of your pussy right now. It seemed like a nigga won a million dollars at the dog track in West Memphis, Arkansas."

"Aahhh, ooohhh. Please, give it to me! Give me my dick now," she said, beating his chest with her small hands.

"You want this big black dick, bitch?" he replied in an aggressive voice that she loved to hear from her man. His sweat dropped from his forehead onto her back. He then inched further into her tight pussy.

"Oohh, yea, player," she moaned, trying to push her ass against him, attempting to stick his whole dick into her pussy. "Please, give me this big black dick, daddy! I need it bad right now, nigga!"

"How bad you want this pipeline?"

"Mmmmm, I-I," she stuttered just as he stroked deeply inside of her, sending chills down her spine. He pulled his dick back out of her pussy and looked down at her creamy nectar that glazed the length of his dick. He slowly stuck the tip of his dick head back inside her pussy. He pulled it back out only to slide it back inside, causing her to whine like a baby. "Please! Please, daddy! Oo-hh my-my fuckin'—ooh!"

"Tell me how bad you want this dick," he whispered, arching his back as he ground the head of his dick in and out of her tight pussy.

"Oohh, I-I-I want. I want it, Tip. Ohh. I—Aahh. Oohhh, I fuckin' need this!" She screamed fiendishly as Keith Sweat's song was playing in the background on her phone, which caused him to switch up his stroke pattern.

"Oh, you need it, Mimi?"

"Yes, yes, yes! I fuckin' need it, baby, in my life!" she screamed, turning her head to the right with a mean scowl on her face, while he deeply thrusted into her drowning wet pussy, as she slowly raised her body.

He was stroking in and out of her pussy so slowly, matching the drums and breakdowns to the beat. Her back quickly gave out as drool dribbled from her bottom lip, numb from the powerful strokes he delivered that released her flow of nectar.

"Ahh. Ahh, fuck!" She groaned out more and more, pulling the pillow to her face more. She bit down into the pillow and growled like a mean pitbull. "I'm cumming, my nigga!"

"Yeah, that's right," he said, stroking even harder as he felt her pussy get wetter, her walls violently contracting around his dick. "Cum all over this big dick, my future wife."

"Aaaaagggghhh!" she bellowed out, as he leaned forward with his left arm wrapped around her midsection, vigorously rubbing her clit in a circular rotation while hitting her with long strokes from Texas to Denver. He was stroking in slow motion, trying to hit all her walls and tame her pussy the way he wanted it to be at the time.

She was trying to run from the extreme chaotic sensation from the combination of her climax and the premeditated strokes of each of his thrust. He continued to rubbed her clit with thirsty, thunderous circular thrusts, causing her eyes to roll into the back of her head while her body experienced slight trembles.

"Damn, nigga, you rock my world on this one. I haven't been fucked by you like this in a long time. You got some good dick, because you fucked a bitch about an hour. You fucked up my weave on my head, as you can see. To be honest, you got my stomach and pussy sore right now. I was running from that dick like I stole something from Walmart and the police were chasing me full speed. I want the chance to be your wife forever. I have so much on my mind at the moment.

"What's that, baby?"

"We will speak about that later down the road before the big dance happens."

Chapter 3

Three years later.

Ebony stood under the warm spray from the shower head, as it beat down on her shoulders and back. She lathered up the loofah and began to wash her breasts one at a time. She took extra care around the areolas, relishing in the sinful sensation that traveled the length of her body. It had been quite a while since her pussy had been with a man, and even as her body craved one's touch, she refused to settle just to get a nut.

She grabbed the nearly empty bottle of Mane 'n Tail shampoo and began lathering her long auburn dreads. It took her almost a full twenty minutes to make sure she had washed them thoroughly, and she knew they would take almost four times as long to dry. On more than one occasion she'd thought about cutting them but could never bring herself to do it. Ebony was rinsing the last of the shampoo out of her hair when the water suddenly became ice-cold. She staggered back, almost slipping in the shower. She quickly adjusted the knobs this way and that way, but the water was still ice-cold.

"You can't be serious!" Ebony huffed. Housing had cut the water . . . again. From the pissy elevators to the abrupt hot water interruptions, Ebony hated public housing. She'd grown up in the part that you had to fight in order to make it around the hood, because somebody was going to take your lunch money and beat your ass for more. She'd thought she was gaining freedom from her parents when she'd left the nest. Had she known what was waiting for her behind door number two, she would've listened to her parents.

Ebony had been the pride of their household. She had an older brother and sister; she was the baby of the family and the one who showed the most promise. Don't forget she liked girls at times when they were alone playing house. Her father was a respected professor at Arkansas State University, and her mother was an RN at Chickasawba Hospital on South Division Street. As a child she wanted for nothing, but her parents also made sure she was kept on a very tight leash. Her father was a devout Muslim, but her mother wasn't, so this often caused conflict in the household. When the issue of religion was raised, her father reluctantly agreed to let the children choose their own path in life, but he always made sure that Islam was present in their home.

Like most young women, Ebony started feeling herself down there when she hit high school. She attended another high school as opposed to Gosnell High School where her parents wanted her to go. They thought she was unable to attend Gosnell because she hadn't been accepted by the school, but unbeknownst to them, Ebony had intercepted the acceptance letter and destroyed it so they'd have to agree to let her go to Mississippi County Community College in Blytheville, Arkansas.

The summer before her junior year, Ebony was a victim of her first crush. He had been a Memphis cat named Peanut, who hustled in the projects near her neighborhood for many years. Peanut had money, cars, and the attention of every girl within a five block radius. Peanut had chased young Ebony for almost six months before she would entertain a small conversation with him about anything. Their courtship went from the chase, to dating, to her being pregnant by the older player.

Her father went through the roof when he found out she was pregnant; had it not been for her mother, he surely would've beaten the baby out of her body. He was angry at his daughter for a long period of time, for deviating from what they'd taught her about being careful, but he was also very hurt. He had watched his own mother struggle to raise him and his lil' sister, and couldn't bear the thought of having his own child throwing her life away. Her father had given her an ultimatum about the child or get out of the house. She decided to leave her parents.

Peanut got them a small apartment on the Westside of town that they could call their own place. The dope game wasn't doing well with him after Moe's crew robbed them and killed several of their crew members. Ebony continued to go to school, but as the baby grew in her stomach, it became more and more of a struggle, and Peanut's moodiness didn't make it any easier. It seemed like the further along she got in her pregnancy, the more distant he became; often she put up with it rather than risk him leaving her. The more she put up with it, the more Peanut's attitude worsened. He even gave her an STD during her six months of pregnancy. When she confronted him about it, he slapped her and accused her of giving it to him from whoring around, even though he was the only man she had ever been with.

Peanut eventually got arrested and left her to take care of the bills and him while he was in jail. She continued to go to school and work a part time job, but the struggles of juggling both of them in her current condition eventually became too much, forcing her to give one up. School wasn't paying her bills, so she let it go and toiled at her job until she was thirty weeks into her pregnancy. She was scared, alone, and broke, but she held it together and gave birth to a beautiful baby boy that she named Tony.

From the first time she held him, she knew that it was impossible to love anyone or anything the way she loved her new son. The first years were the roughest for them, with Ebony having to go without eating some nights so that her son would. Just before Tony's third birthday, she got the news that Peanut had been released from federal prison, but for some reason he hadn't bothered to tell her that he was getting out. She found out through a nephew that he was staying with his parents in Gosnell, Arkansas. So, one rainy day, she bundled little Tony up and drove the short trip up to Gosnell.

She wanted to surprise Peanut, but she was the one who ended up being surprised when she showed up on the doorstep only to find Peanut living with another bitch who was also pregnant by his low down ass. Peanut looked at her like she was the dirt on the bottom of his shoes, and told his new girlfriend that she was just an obsessed little girl who was trying to pin another man's baby on him. Ebony showed him what it meant to *obsessed*, when she opened his forearm up with a box cutter. That was the last time she saw Peanut. Her first crush had changed and damaged her heart beyond repair, so Ebony threw herself into raising her son and trying to get her life back together. From that moment on, she vowed that the only man she would ever let into her heart again was her son Tony.

Ebony hadn't realized that she was crying until she blinked and a tear rolled down her cheek. She laughed because her tears were warmer than the water in the shower. Ignoring the frigid cold, Ebony hurriedly washed away the rest of the shampoo and soap and jumped out of the shower so she could finish getting dressed. With towels wrapped around her nice body and hair, she stepped out of the bathroom and tripped over a sneaker that had been carelessly left in the hallway.

"Damn it, Tony," she cursed, snatching the sneaker up and making her way down the short hallway to his bedroom. Tony was growing up fast. Before she reached the door, she could hear the music coming from the room. Ebony pushed the door open and looked at her son in a state of shock.

At eleven years old Tony was almost as tall as Ebony but weighed only 80 pounds. He was dressed in a red black label t-shirt she'd bought him for Christmas, and a pair of skinny jeans with a red bandana hanging from his back pocket. He never heard Ebony walk into the room, but he felt it when she suddenly smacked him upside the head.

"What the fuck," Tony started but caught himself. "Ma, why you hit me upside the head for?"

"You're lucky I didn't punch you in the damn mouth." She snatched the bandana. "What the hell is this, little nigga?"

"Huh?" Tony asked dumbly.

Ebony grabbed him by the front of his t-shirt and hauled him in close. "Boy, don't play with me. What are you doing carrying this damn flag?" Ebony gave him another pop with the hand, holding the sweat rag. "Tony, you know I ain't no square bitch, so cut it out, okay? The people and things you choose to identify yourself with have life-altering consequences, especially this little game right there." She waved the flag in his face. "In certain neighborhoods this piece of cloth could cost you your life in a heartbeat. I'll kill myself before I let the streets take you, baby. Do you understand?"

Tony looked at the flag, as if he were seeing it for the first time. "That ain't no flag, ma, flags have stripes and stars. That's just an old sweat rag."

"Where did you get those tight ass jeans, because I know I didn't buy them." She frowned at the jeans. "No, I don't like them. Boy, it looks like you're wearing spandex." Ebony tugged at the jeans, but they had no give.

"Ma, you bugging. All the kids wearing these," Tony told her.

"Well, not my boy," she shot back. "Change them jeans before you give yourself a yeast infection." She snapped the bandana at him playfully and left the room.

Twenty minutes later, they were both dressed and ready to face the world. As soon as Ebony and Tony stepped into the hallway, they smelled it. It was like the smell of burning paper, with an acidic bite. Ebony sighed and made her way to Stairwell B and peeked inside. Then she shoved the door to Stairwell C open and scared the daylights out of Blunt, who nearly dropped the crack pipe he was smoking on.

"Damn it, Blunt!" Ebony snapped.

"Girl, you know better than to be sneaking up on me like that. I'm an old player." Blunt gave her a rotten-toothed grin. He was dressed in a business suit and dirty overcoat. At one time Blunt had been a master booster, but now he was just another addict trying to escape the reality of his life.

"You know better than to be smoking that shit on my floor. I asked y'all not to do that." Ebony folded her small arms.

"Come on, baby girl, it's cold on the streets." Blunt pulled his jacket collar up as if the chill had suddenly made it inside the stairwell.

"Then smoke them rocks in your own damn house."

Blunt gave her a bewildered look. "And have my mama kill me? I don't think so, baby. Other than busting the balls of honest crackheads like myself, what you been up to, Ebony?"

"Trying to keep crackheads from trying to get high in my stairway," she joked. "Nah, I'm just out here trying to get in where I fit in."

"Ebony, girls like you don't fit in, you carve your own niches. You ain't like the rest of these little women."

"Blunt, how do you figure that and we all live in the same nasty ass projects?" she asked.

"Because you've got the good sense to see outside these project bricks," he replied. "Ebony, I know you ain't no angel, but you ain't into all kinds of foolishness like the rest of these bitches. I watched the young girls floating around these projects from sun up to sun down keeping company with different men and cussing like they ain't got no sense."

"Blunt, one could question your sense for still smoking them crack rocks," she said.

He looked at the pipe that he had only just realized that he was still holding and shrugged. "Old habits for an old fool like me. You know how shit can be."

"Ma, elevator!" Tony called. He was holding the elevator door open and tapping his foot impatiently.

"I'll catch you later, Blunt." Ebony waved and got into the elevator.

The tiny steel car was hot, greasy, and rank as it was most of the time. Shit had got rough with Ebony to the point she had to move into the project and start from the bottom. Ebony and her son had to stand nearly pressed against the door to avoid stepping in the puddle of urine in the center of the elevator. It seemed like no matter what time of day or night Ebony came in, they were the few who were just trouble, which was the case with the young boy holding the door for Ebony and Tony.

"What's good, fam?" Kush gave little Tony dap. The kids' eyes lit up.

"Tony. His name is Tony," Ebony repeated.

"My fault, babe girl, I didn't mean nothing by it," Kush told her with a crooked grin on his face.

"It's all good." She took Tony by the hand and hurried toward the avenue. "I want you to stay away from that boy, do you hear me?" she told Tony once they were out of earshot.

"Kush is cool. That's the big homie," Tony said proudly.

"That snake ass nigga is not your homie, and I'd better not catch you in that lobby with him and the rest of those young delinquents. Do you hear me, Tony?"

"Okay, *doing*," Tony grumbled. He knew that his mother rode him to protect him, but he hated when she treated him like some stupid kid who didn't know what was happening on the streets. In Tony's mind he was technically the man of the house; therefore, it was his job to make sure his family was good. Day in and day out, he watched his mother struggle just so that they could have a little, and it tore him apart inside. He vowed that one day she would be able to just kick her feet up while he took care of things.

As they stood on the curb waiting for the light to change so that they could cross the street and catch the number four bus, a green Honda pulled to a clumsy stop at the curb. The door flew open, releasing a cloud of weed smoke and profane lyrics that were blasting from the speaker. A girl slithered from the car dressed in a pair of tight-fitting Chanel jeans and spandex shirt. She had a bit of a gut, but her small waist and curvaceous hips drew attention away from it. The light breeze blew her rich red weave, making her look like the fake Lil' Kim at a photoshoot. In her manicured hand she held the 6-inch heels that had given her feet enough hell so that she wore her broke down thong flip-flops in the chill. Between her Chanel-coated lips she twirled an apple lollipop back and forth while the driver gave her his parting words. She laughed and blew him a kiss, releasing him from her spell and allowing him to compose himself enough to drive away. Keisha Daniels was a bad bitch. She dared anyone to tell her differently.

"What's up, Keisha? I'm surprised to see your ass out and about so early," Ebony greeted her.

"Girl, I'm just coming in," Keisha said proudly. "What's up, Tony? Boy, you're getting just as big and fine as you wanna be." She smiled at him, showing off the twenty-six grand dental work she'd had done.

"Yeah, I know you see me, Keisha, but you need to see about me," Tony capped.

Keisha laughed. "Listen to this one."

"You better watch that mouth of yours." Ebony pointed her finger at her son.

"It's all good, Ebony. You know it'll be years before his little ass even has an idea of what to do with all this pussy." She then slapped herself on the ass cheeks.

"I doubt if he'll be able to handle you even then. Where are you coming from this morning?"

Keisha popped the lollipop from her mouth. She waved it like a conductor's wand as she spoke. "Girl, ole boy from the Lilly Street Mafia had a party in Memphis TN. A friend of a friend had the hookup, so you know I had to be in the building. It was something in the building that caught my attention. I hit your phone to see if you wanted to roll, but when you didn't answer, I ended up having to take that dusty bitch Sarah with me, and you know the girl ain't got no home training."

"I was probably studying when you called me, bitch; you know I don't take no phone calls during crunch time," she reminded her.

"You still taking them online classes?"

"Five months away from an Associates in Business Management."

"Ebony, you're better than me, bitch. After spending twelve years in school I couldn't see myself doing another day let alone two more years just to get some piece of paper that says I'm qualified to do something that a bitch already knows how to do anyway."

"That piece of white paper is gonna be me and my little man's ticket outta these bricks," Ebony said.

"There's easier ways to getting outta the projects than busting your brain with those books. Paying the white government back for the money you had to borrow to get the ball rolling in the first place. Bitches like you hustle backward once they fall off, Ebony. You're beautiful, smart, so it wouldn't be nothing for you to find somebody willing to lighten that load of yours and take you up outta here. You just gotta know how to go about it."

"Keisha, you're three times as pretty as me and you've been in these projects all your life," Ebony pointed out.

"That's by choice, baby-boo. I've lived in plenty of places, but it ain't nothing like my projects. Look, my whole entire family is here so I ain't never got a problem with a babysitter, and the fact that I ain't gotta pay no light or gas bill frees up money for other shit."

Ebony thought on it. "But don't you get tired of all the bullshit that comes with living here? Kush and his boys play the lobby twenty-four-seven. If I had a dollar for every time the hot water was cut off or the elevator were broken, I'd be a rich bitch. I'm not knocking what you're saying, Keisha, but I don't think I could spend the rest of my life living off the mercies of public assistance and this jacked up ass housing system."

"Now hold on, little Ms. Cupcake." Keisha placed her hands on her hips and looked at Ebony seriously. "I've worked several jobs since I was nine years old. Even when I got pregnant with my son, I had a gig downtown. I've given the state enough of my damn time and hard earned money, so it's only right that they returned the favor. For as long as the state is knocking out the bulk of my rent, I ain't got too much other than read and dress," Keisha said with a snap of her fingers.

"A bitch feels you, Keisha, but I'd still rather go get it than have it given to me."

"Which is why your ass is broke and man-less now," Keishia teased her. "But on the real, I ain't mad at you for the moves you're making, Ebony. If I had as high a tolerance for bullshit as you do, then I might not be out here living by my wits now."

"It ain't never too late, Keisha."

"Yeah, but I think I'm gonna have fun with it for a while. Let me take my ass upstairs so I can lie down. I aint' been to sleep in almost seventy-two hours," Keisha said.

"Do you, and I'll catch you later. You still gonna be able to style my hair tonight?" Ebony twirled a handful of her locks.

"Yeah, as long as you come by at a decent time. I heard my cuz is in town and I'm trying to catch up with her before she breezes again."

"I ain't seen Loud crazy ass in a minute, what up with her? Does she still date that drug dealer?" Ebony asked.

"Yeah, she still all wifed up to that crazy muthafucka. Cuzo sure picked a live one with him. I don't even try to understand their relationship, but I'm loving the benefits she gets from being a baller's wifey. I'm trying to get her to hook me up with one of them niggas be having all the money and more material shit."

Ebony shook her head. "Keisha, I don't know how you balance your children in this rock and roll lifestyle of yours."

Keisha winked her eye at her. "It's an art, baby. Maybe one day when you come up for air outta them books I can give you a lesson or two." Keisha rubbed Tony's cheek as she passed him. "Bye, handsome."

"Imma holla at you later," Tony blushed.

"Boy, bring your thirsty ass on." Ebony snatched him by the arm to the bus stop. This shit was crazy to Ebony because she was not used to living in the project and not being able to handle her own. She had lost everything and got to start over from the bottom. She couldn't help but think whether she should venture into the dope game or find a high-paying job that will support her and Tony.

Chapter 4

Keisha walked up to the block, sucking her apple lollipop and switching her ass hard enough to dislocate her hips. She turned the attention of just about everyone she passed, including the females. As she cut down the path en route to the stairs leading to her apartments, she spotted two local stoop rats sitting on the bench, sharing a Newport cigarette. The one rocking the head gear and mean-mug was named Purple. She was a brown-skinned girl with a loveable body, but a face that took a special kind of love or several shots to stare at for too long. Purple was washed up, but thought that she still had a shot at greatness. With three kids by almost as many hardcore niggas, it was a jump off. Keisha couldn't stand Purple and the only reason she hadn't whipped her out yet was because she was one of the friends of her cousin, Loud. What someone of Loud's caliber could see in a girl like Purple was beyond Keisha's comprehension, but she let it be to keep the peace.

The second girl wasn't a hard-faced baby-making machine with a chip on her shoulder, but she was no less trifling. With big wide eyes and inviting smile, she had the face of an angel and the wit of a snake. Cloud was a pretty light-skinned girl who had moved to the project from Memphis, Tennessee. She had fled to Arkansas due to the murder that a woman was found dead at the scene of what the cops were calling a drug deal gone bad. For a long period of time she floated from borough to borough doing what she could to survive, until she had managed to locate some cousins of hers who were living in the projects and opened their home to her. It didn't take long for her to get a taste of the darker side of Blytheville, Arkansas life and became turned out. She was a young girl with Champagne dreams and beer money, but considering what she came from, she was doing okay for herself.

Cloud waved and Keisha waved back. They knew some of the same people, so they were cordial when they saw each other, but not Purple. She shot daggers at Keisha as she passed, to which Keisha responded by throwing on her Chanel shades and switching her hips harder. To Keisha, Purple's was just one more sour face in a world of many.

Ever since Keisha could remember, she and her family had lived a world apart from their neighbors in the projects. With all the dirt they were involved in, it was the safest way to avoid an indictment. Keisha was descended from a very long line of criminals. The Daniels Family notoriety went all the way back to her grandfather Junebug, who in his heyday had been a leg breaker for Sally Williams but became the local numbers man in his later years. Up until the time of his death, Junebug Jr. had been the man for many years since the death of his father Junebug Sr. It was a fixation that he passed on to all of his sons, but Junebug Jr. showed the most promise. He was a beast when it came to his grind and his woman—Jazz—was no slouch either. They were like the Bonnie and Clyde of the late eighties, and they lavished everything they took in on their baby girl, Keisha.

During her development years, Keisha stumbled through life, making more than her fair share of bad decisions, especially when it came to men. Keisha had always been a beautiful girl, so men were constantly coming at her, promising everything but delivering nothing. She had to make trips to planned parenthood and the free clinic more often than she cared to remember, before she even got a clue as to sorting bullshit from the truth. For as hard as her aunts and uncles had made her mentally, there wasn't much they could do about her tender heart. The more she had gotten her heart broken, the colder she became, until it reached a point where she just stopped feeling anything at all. By the time Keisha was able to stand on her own, she had become a predator and everything was flood.

"What's up, Keisha?" Kush called from the stairs. He had his henchman Cash with him.

"About to turn it in because I'm tired as hell." She continued walking toward the building with the three stooges on her heels.

"I know that's right because you've been running through my mind all day," Cash said. He was a funny-faced, dark-skinned kid with an overbite and a nervous tick.

"Oh, now that's one I never heard before," Keisha said sarcastically. She tapped for the elevator and busied herself with her Blackberry, hoping they'd get the hint, which they didn't.

Kush stepped up before Cash could hit her with another stupid line. "So what you getting into today?"

"My bad, I just told you that I'm tired." Keisha rolled her eyes behind her shades. She silently wished that the elevator would hurry so she could get away from Kush. She'd known him for years, but he still gave the creeps.

Kush scowled. "Yeah, I forgot that you run in high-class circles."

"Because I'm a high-class bitch. Ask about me," Keisha said, waving her lollipop dismissively.

"A'ight, so if not a movie then let's go get something to eat," Kush pressed her.

The elevator was still nowhere in sight and Keisha couldn't take any more so she decided to level with him. "Look," she removed her Chanel shades, "Kush, you my nigga, but you know I ain't messing with you like that."

"And what's that supposed to mean?" he asked.

"Nothing, it just means that I ain't really got time for the bullshit you're putting down. Me and you live two different lifestyles."

"Oh, so now you acting all high off ya shit cuz you shining a little bit? I guess you too good to fuck with the hood niggas anymore?" Kush asked defensively.

"Never that, you know my family is filled with some of the illest niggas this project or any other has yet to produce. What I'm saying is that you still running around trying to game bitches outta their drawer with a small bag of weed and that ain't me, player."

"There you go with that bullshit." Kush sucked his teeth.

"No, there you go with that bullshit. Kush, you shit where you live so your dirt is out there for everyone to see. Why do you think ain't nobody in the hood fucking with you but them snow bunnies bitches?"

"Keisha, you know how the streets talk."

"Nah, I know how you move, nigga. Kush, me and you are people but ain't gonna never be much more than that," she told him just as the elevator finally reached the first floor. Keisha stepped into the car without as much as a goodbye.

"Well, fuck you too then, black bitch," Kush said after the elevator door had closed.

"Damn, I would love to have her work my dick like she be working them lollipops," Cash said.

"Keisha ain't trying to fuck with you, nigga. You're a scumbag," Kush told him.

"Well, she ain't fucking with you either, so that make us scumbags. And if Sam ever caught wind that we sniffing around his baby mother, he might not appreciate it."

Kush looked at Cash like he was stupid. "Nigga, is you crazy? They gave Sam the long haul in federal prison. That fast bitch Keisha ain't fit to be no prisoner's wife. If it ain't my dick that tames her, it'll be some other nigga that's out here getting it. With a bitch like Keisha, you can fuck her anytime of the week, but if you ain't handling, it ain't gonna get you no closer to your heart, because she ain't got one." Kush pushed past Cash and walked back outside. When he emerged from the building, Cloud and Purple were still sitting on the bench. He looked at the girls who were staring at him in anticipation and figured something was better than nothing. "What up? Y'all trying to get high?"

***

Ebony was dead on her feet by the time she came out of the bus station. She had been out since that morning pounding the pavement and filling out job applications with anyone who said they were hiring. She'd been at it at least four times a week for the last month or so and still hadn't landed anything. Having to take care of herself and Tony, she was feeling the pinch of the dwindling economy, and what little she got from public assistance wasn't doing much to ease it. The only reason she still bothered with them is because it kept her freezer stocked. Thinking of her food stamps made her remember that she still hadn't gotten anything for dinner. As bad as her feet were hurting, the supermarket seemed like it was miles away. She decided that it would be easier just to grab some cold cut sandwiches and call it a night, so she headed for the corner deli on the block.

As she was approaching the deli, she spotted a familiar face unloading some crates off a delivery truck. She started to turn around and go the other way, but before she could move he had already spotted her. He was ruggedly handsome with chocolate skin and wavy black hair that blended nicely into his neat beard. His name was Smoke, and he was one of the guys who made the weekly deliveries to the local bodega, and this was another impulsive decision she regretted.

Ebony and Smoke had flirted heavily for about a month or so before they started officially seeing each other. He was slightly older and therefore a bit more seasoned and had her open with things like Broadway plays and nice dinners.

Being as inexperienced with life and men as she was, she found herself falling for him and giving her body to him. When they had sex, Smoke took her body to heights that Peanut had never even come close to, and she lavished as much of her young pussy on him as he could stand. After a while, she began noticing subtle hints that something was wrong, when it became harder to get him on the phone and his visits became less frequent. When she'd started hearing the rumors of him having another bitch on the side, she tried not to feed into them, but she couldn't deny the writing on the wall. She wasn't foolish enough to wait around until the other shoe dropped, so she cut him loose and changed her phone number. She still bumped into him from time to time when he was making deliveries but she always kept the conversations short and sweet.

"What's good, stranger?" He greeted her with a warm smile. He had to have paid a grip for his teeth because they were perfect and white.

She shrugged shyly. "Same old, same old. I can't really complain," she said and reached for the door, but he stopped her by placing his large hand against it.

"Damn, it's like that?"

"It ain't like nothing, Smoke. What are you talking about?"

"I'm talking about how you just left a nigga hanging with no explanation. I thought we had something going?"

"We did have something, but you didn't want it unless it was on your terms, remember?" She reminded him.

"It wasn't like that and you know it."

She folded her small arms. "So what was it like, Smoke? Come on, I'm a big girl so you ain't gotta lie to me, player. You wanted to do your thing so I gave you enough space to do it."

He sighed. "Ebony, I ain't gonna front like I wasn't doing my thing, but you know you were always special to me." He pulled her in for a nice hug.

Ebony tried to push away, but he held fast. Don't start this shit, Smoke." She breathed deeply of his scent. He was a little musty from working all day, but she could smell the sweetness of baby powder lingering beneath.

"I ain't trying to start nothing. I'm trying to finish it. Why don't we go to dinner tonight and have a small talk?"

For an instant Ebony considered it, but quietly pushed the thought from her mind. "Nah, that ain't gonna work." She broke the embrace and walked into the store.

Ebony greeted the old man sitting on a crate by the front door and shouted her order to the dude behind the counter. Smoke was in the back having the owner sign for the deliveries, so she wanted to get her stuff and get out as quickly as possible. She could feel Smoke's eyes on her as she tried to decide between onion and garlic chips or barbecue, but she wouldn't give him or her the satisfaction of looking up at him. She didn't trust herself, especially her eyes. The eyes would always be the giveaway. Pushing the silliness out of her head, she grabbed her snacks and headed to the counter where the young man was just finishing up her sandwiches. Living in the hood may have had its disadvantages, but there was nothing like a heated roast beef and cheddar from the corner store.

"Twenty-four-seven-three altogether, Miss," the dude behind the counter told her.

Ebony peeked over her shoulder to make sure Smoke wasn't watching, before pulling her Quest card out of her purse and sliding it through the machine and punching in her PIN. The young man at the counter looked down at the machine and after a few seconds frowned.

"It didn't go through. Maybe you should try it again?" he suggested. She swiped her card again but it still didn't perform right. "I don't know," he said with a shrug.

"That's impossible, let me try it once more," she said in a soft voice.

43

"You already tried it twice and it didn't work. You gotta either pay cash or I can't help you."

She fished around in her purse and only came up with five dollars. Even if she put all the snacks back, she still wouldn't have enough to cover the sandwiches. She felt like melting into a puddle of shit because she had no idea what they were going to eat until she had a chance to find out what was going on with her credit card the next morning. She felt someone hovering over her and turned to see Smoke. The incident had gone from bad to worse.

"Here you go, Ock." Smoke handed him a hundred-dollar bill. Just give my change to the lady." He strode for the front door.

Ebony looked from the total to Smoke's parting back. Reluctantly, she snatched the hundred-dollar bill and caught him at the door. "Nah, I'm straight." She tried to hand him the money back but he refused to take it.

"It's all good, Ebony. Just get your food," he told her.

"I ain't no charity case!" she blurted out and immediately regretted it when she saw the pity in his eyes. "What I mean is, I don't like owing nobody shit."

"And I don't like to be owed, which is why it was a gift," he replied and continued walking out of the store toward his Range Rover.

Ebony wanted to let it go, but her pride told her that there was more to say, so she followed. "It's never nothing for something. Even doctors get paid to save lives. I really appreciate what you're doing, Smoke, but if you don't let me pay you back then it's gonna bother me."

Smoke thought on it for a minute. "Okay, if you insist on paying me back let's hook up tonight."

"I don't think that would be a good idea," she said.

"Stop acting like that, Ebony. I ain't asking for no pussy. I just wanna hang out for a while. I missed you, baby," he said sincerely.

Ebony entertained it briefly, then caught herself. "Nah, besides, I've got little man."

"If not tonight then maybe tomorrow, or the day after?" He pressed.

"Smoke—"

"Ebony, you said yourself that if you owe me it's gonna bother you." He smirked.

Looking at that perfect white smile took her somewhere else. "I'll think about it and get back with you on it."

"A'ight, fair enough. So let me get your phone number and—"

"Stop it, I said I'd call you."

"Okay, okay, I ain't gonna twist your arm about it, sis." Smoke climbed into his Range Rover and rolled the front window to conclude their conversation. "I know you said you can't make it out tonight, but I hope you change your mind and heart. It's veal night at Club Tubb's on the east side of town and you know how you love that fire weed."

"Whatever, Smoke." She smiled. "I'll call you."

"Make sure you handle that, babe. Make sure you do that." Smoke winked and pulled the truck out into traffic.

She stood there until the Range Rover had disappeared up Lake Avenue and only when she was sure he could no longer see her did she smile. Smoke could be a snake like the rest of them, but he always made her feel special when they were together and that's what she loved the most about him. She doubted that she would take Smoke up on his invitation, but it still felt good for someone to offer. After getting her sandwiches, she made her way to her side of the projects. She replayed the conversation over in her head, holding on to the small moment of elation. Her heart told her that nothing could ruin her day, but when she made it to the front of her building she knew that her heart had been wrong . . . again.

Chapter 5

Tony got off the bus at Williams Park on the east side of town and bounced up the stairs to the Avenue. When he emerged from the station, he gave a cautious look around to make sure nobody saw him for fear that they would tell his mother. She had only recently started allowing him to travel by himself via public transportation, and that was only after he promised to only take the bus to and from school. She was fearful of all the craziness that went on the city bus, but all the kids from his school were cool and he didn't want to be the square.

Along his walk up to the project it seemed like Tony must've waved hello to at least a dozen people before he finally crossed over into the projects. He and his mother were very well liked among most of the people because they treated everyone with respect no matter what walk of life they came from. Ebony had always instilled this trait in her son, and she would go upside his head whenever he strayed from it. When he rounded the corner of his building, he saw his friend—Gantsa—posted up in the building with Kush. Tony pushed his pants down slightly off his ass and threw an extra bop in his walk as he approached.

"You see, little nigga, that's the kinda shit you gotta be heartless out here or these folks are gonna walk all over you," Kush was telling Gantsa when Tony walked up.

"What's up, y'all, what's going on?" Tony gave everyone in front of the building some dap.

"Ain't nothing, just schooling ya lil' man on the laws of the game," Kush said proudly. "What's popping though?"

"Ain't nothing, just coming from school," Tony said.

"Where it's at is upstairs for you, little one. You know your mother would trip if she caught you out here with the hard legs," King told him. King was the elder statesman among the young homies on the block. His crew supplied Kush and several other low-level players with the poison they slung in the hood. King was a quiet man who practiced love over war, but his name had been tied to a few dead bodies.

Tony looked at the other heads that were snickering and addressed King. "Come on, man, why you acting like I'm doing something wrong by standing in front of the building I live in?"

King saw that Kush and the others were watching so he was mindful of his words so as not to bruise young Tony's ego. "Tony, I ain't trying to stop your shine, but you know what we do around here, so the block is always hot, player. The police or feds could roll up at any given moment and cart us all off to the county jail or the slammer."

"Damn, King, all you talking about is getting caught. I'd be more worried about making money than the folks," Cash said boastfully.

"Which is why your simple ass is always getting pinched for something stupid," King shot back. "My nigga, with all the shit they're building up and down the hood how long do you think they're gonna let you be out here making it jump? Nah, the block is five times as hot and the money is half as long."

"Well, if it's that then how come you still hustle, King?" Tony asked.

The question caught King off guard, so he decided to answer it as honestly as he could. "Because it's all I know. Look, we get it how we live because these are the cards society dealt us, but you come from something else, Tony.

Your mother makes sure you're taken care of so you ain't gotta be out here playing yourself."

"Man, that little bit of money we get from welfare ain't doing nothing. There's gonna come a time when I gotta step my game up, player," Tony said.

"Then you step your game up by sticking to the plans your mother has laid out for you instead of trying to get caught up out here with theses niggas," King said a little more sharply than he'd intended to. Seeing the hurt in the boy's face, he softened his tone. "Tony, I ain't trying to come down on you, I'm just trying to let you know what's popping."

"Shit, he lives in the projects like the rest of us so I'm sure he knows what it is out here. Let the little nigga be." Kush sucked his teeth. He hated when King started preaching.

King shot him a dirty look then turned his attention back to Tony. "My G, stay a kid for a while and leave this here business to the grown people."

Ebony stormed up. "Tony, what are you doing hanging out in front of this building?"

"What up, Ebony?" Kush greeted her with a smile.

"Not now, Kush," Ebony said, never taking her eyes off her son who was standing there nervously. "Tony, I asked you a question."

"I was just chilling for a minute," Tony mumbled.

"Chilling my ass. I told you I don't want you hanging in front of this hot ass apartments!"

"Ebony, he only been here for a second or two and I was just sending him upstairs." King tried to advocate for Tony, which turned her anger on him.

"King, you stick to telling the rest of these little dudes what to do and I'll handle my own child, thank you very much," Ebony said with attitude. "And does your aunt know you're out here?" She turned to Gantsa.

Gantsa shrugged. "I don't think she'd care too much if she did."

Ebony sighed. "Let's go, Tony." She snatched the door open. As Tony walked into the apartment, he cut his eyes at her and was rewarded with a hard slap in the back of the head. "You roll them eyes at me again and I'll pluck them outta your damn head." She pushed him. King and the others could still hear Ebony yelling at Tony after the heavy door had closed.

"Man, she straight spazzed on that little nigga." Kush laughed and gave his boys a high five.

King looked at him and shook his head. "Kush, you ain't shit for laughing at Tony like that for his mom going in on him. I keep telling you that it's bad business to have these young boys out here with you."

Kush sucked his teeth. "Man, why you coming at me like I'm making these little dudes stand around out here? If they wanna play the block and get a little change then that's on their parents to tell them differently. Me, I'm trying to let everybody eat who wants to get a dollar."

"Which is why one of these bitches is either gonna call the police on you or cut your fucking throat over their kids," King warned.

"Well, I don't recall you kicking that *save the children* shit when you gave me my first bundle," Kush shot back.

"We're a different breed of niggas, Kush. We took to the streets because we were starving and this was the only way to feed ourselves."

"And what do you think is going on with the next generation?" Kush challenged. "Damn near every bitch in the hood is either on welfare or some kind of government help, getting peanuts a month, so their kids look to the streets to get their money up. If you wanna blame somebody, then blame their mamas for lying on their asses collecting government checks instead of trying to work somewhere."

King shook his head. "You just don't get it, do you?"

"Nope," Kush said smugly.

"Fuck it, I'm out." King gave Kush dap. Cash extended his hand but King looked at him as if he was stupid and walked off.

"Bitch ass nigga," Cash said once King was out of earshot.

"Man, the only reason King is acting all concerned over this little nigga is because he wants to smash Ebony," Kush said scornfully.

"Shorty do got a large ass on her. I had thought about fucking that myself," Cash said.

"Please, that uppity bitch ain't trying to give your project ass no pussy. For as long as she's been living here I don't know not one nigga that she let smash."

"Maybe she likes pussy," Cash suggested.

"Maybe, but once she gets a shot of this horse dick, she's gonna come back over to this side." Kush grabbed his dick. He suddenly noticed Gantsa giving him a disturbing look. "What, you tight because I'm talking about your man's moms?"

"Nah, I'm straight," Gantsa lied. He really wanted to bust Kush in his head for talking about Ebony in such a way. Ever since he and Tony had become friends, Ebony had treated him as if he was her own son. When his mother would go on her drug binges, it was Ebony who would take him in and make sure that he was fed and off the streets.

"Yeah, you're cool, alright. Now get your cool ass to work and get that bag up you let Shakes burn you for. I'm about to shoot 'cross town right quick and get something to eat."

"Yeah, I'm hungry than a muthafucka too," Cash said.

"Then you better go up the block to the nearest store and get a special because your ass is staying out here with Gantsa. I don't need no more fuckups."

"Why I gotta stay out here with him?" Cash complained.

"Because I said so. Now stop crying like a little hoe and let's get this money," Kush told him before walking off.

"Damn, why that nigga always serious?" Gantsa asked once Kush had gone.

"Because this shit ain't a game out here, which is what we keep trying silly little muthafuckers like you," Cash snapped. "Player, if you plan on living long enough to see a dollar, you better wise up to what the fuck is good in the streets. The fact that your ass is out here pitching in front of the apartment says that you're behind the curve already.

"But you're out here with me, so where does that put you on the curve?" Gantsa shot back.

"You a real funny dude, you know that." Cash leaned against the gate and lit a cigarette. He took deep drags off his square, ignoring Gantsa, and scoped the scenery. When his eyes landed on the two figures creeping toward him, he choked on the smoke. "Shit," he began coughing.

"You good?" Gantsa asked in a genuinely concerned voice.

"Hell nawl, nigga. Let's take a walk," Cash urged.

"Hold on, player, don't dip off just yet." Big Face's voice froze the fleeing dealers. He was dressed in a forest sweat suit and matching suede Nikes. The flap of his do-rag blew in the breeze like a flag on a pole. On his heels was his brutish partner, Chris. Chris looked like a walking mailbox with a nappy afro and a lazy eye. He wasn't the sharpest knife in the kitchen, but deadly in combat.

"Oh, shit, what up, Face? I didn't even see you," Cash lied.

"Umm-humm," Face said, sucking his teeth and eyeing Cash suspiciously. "What the business is, youngster?"

Cash laughed nervously. "Nothing much, man. Just out here chilling, you know?"

Chris snorted. "Look like they out here clocking dollars to me, Face."

Face raised an eyebrow. "Is that right? Y'all little niggas out here getting money? If that's the case, then let me hold something."

Cash patted his pockets and shrugged. "I ain't got a dime."

Big Face's eye narrowed to slits. "Y'all out here selling crack all day and don't have any money? That shit sounds kinda funny to me." Big Face sucked his teeth. "Real funny, my nigga." Face looked at Gantsa, who looked like he would piss on himself at any moment. "A'ight, so we gonna play a little game called *I find all I keep.*"

"Man, Face, I ain't gonna have you out here patting me down like I'm still ten years old. This is a brand new day," Cash said defiantly.

Big Face raised his shirt so that Cash could see the butt of the .44 handgun he was carrying. "New day, same nigga. Now grab the muthafucking ceiling before I disrespect you out here," Face ordered and began patting Cash down. From Cash's pocket he produced a wad of money. "Umm-hmmm, thought you ain't have it?"

"Come on, that's the pack money," Cash said.

"It was the re-up money. Now it's a street tax for you lying to me." Face laughed at him. "Now where the crack at?"

"If Cash got the money then this little nigga is probably holding the rocks." Chris shoved Gantsa toward Big Face.

"What's up with it?" Big Face asked Gantsa. Gantsa looked at the floor and said nothing. "Small nigga, I'd hate to have cut them big ass pussy lips of yours to prove a point. Cough up the rocks," Big Face barked. Keeping his eyes on the ground, Gantsa handed over the bag full of crack he had hidden in his pants. "What's this about a G-pack?" Big Face tested the weight. "Yeah, this is nice. Looks like we gonna have us a great old welcome home celebration tonight, Chris."

"Sho nuff, Big Face, sho nuff," Chris said happily.

"Big Face gave him a comical look. "Pussy, you ain't gonna bust a grape in the Welch backyard. And if that Scarface sissy you work for wants to make something of it,

I'll be right on West Rose smoking your crack." Big Face bopped off with Chris in tow. As an afterthought he turned to Gantsa. "Young man, if I were you I'd find a better class of friends to hang out with because these niggas gonna fuck around and get you murdered around here. Find yourself another game because you damn sure ain't got the heart to play this one."

Cash continued staring up the block long after Big Face and Chris disappeared into the building. If he'd had a gun he would've shot Big Face dead, but since he wasn't strapped all he could do was stand there and fume, wondering how he was going to break the news to Kush that they'd taken another loss in the dope game.

Chapter 6

Kush laid back on the tattered bar stool blowing rings of smoke through his nose and watching them dissipate into the air. Between his legs Purple knelt on a soft cushion staring up at him with weed slanted eyes. In one hand she held a twenty-two-ounce of Miller Lite and in the other hand his large dick.

"You know I don't be doing this kinda shit, right?" she asked, taking a sip of her beer.

"I know, baby, and that's why I'm gonna make sure you're taken care of," Kush assured her, gently running his fingers through her sloppy weave.

Purple hesitated for a minute before she finally allowed him to guide her head down to his waiting dick. When she closed her mouth around the head, he hissed like a rattlesnake that had just been disturbed from an afternoon nap. She teased the rim of his dick with the tip of her sharp tongue, occasionally licking down the base of his hard dick.

"Damn, this shit is good," Kush panted. Gantsa, come get some of this pussy."

"Nah, I'm good." Gantsa stood in the corner looking like he was about to audition for American Idol. He was a young thug nigga, who wasn't much older than Tony, but dying to prove to the older niggas that he belonged.

"Let me find out this nigga is scared of pussy." Cash snickered from the kitchen table where he was weighing cocaine and baking soda that had to be cooked.

"Fuck you, nigga, I ain't scared," Gantsa said in a very unconvincing tone. He had never been with a woman, but he wouldn't tell them that and leave himself open for further ridicule from his new friends.

Kush continued to manipulate Purple's head and regarded Gantsa with a critical eye. "Shorty, I know you ain't in her talking scared business? You talked all that bullshit about getting bread on the block and you scared to hit some pussy?" Kush shook his head. Maybe you ain't ready to play with the big boys."

"Nawl, I'm ready to get it with, y'all," Gantsa said.

A tremor went through Kush as Purple took all of him in her deep throat and tickled his balls with her tongue ring. "If you're ready then you need to get over here and handle your business." Kush tossed Gantsa a colorful condom.

Gantsa stood there staring at the condom and the thick ass hiked up in front of him. The prospect of mounting Purple made him so nervous that he felt his bowels shift. He looked from Kush's judgmental expression to the golden tunnel in front of him and knew what he had to do. With trembling hands Gantsa slipped the condom on and eased behind Purple with his pants around his ankles. When he entered her from behind, the heat of her pussy radiated through him as if someone had trapped a little piece of the sun and stuck it up inside her. As Gantsa stroked her, he fought to keep his cool, but it was a losing battle and he ended up blowing his wad in less than four minutes. Gantsa got up and duck-waddled to the kitchen.

Purple took Kush's dick from her mouth and looked over her shoulder at Gantsa who was cleaning himself with a wet t-shirt. "Damn, either my pussy is just that good or your little ass is a virgin."

"Bitch, I ain't no virgin," Gantsa said heatedly.

"Hey, watch your fucking mouth, little nigga," Kush told Gantsa. "And you stop fucking with my little soldier and get back to work on my big man," he told Purple and shoved his dick back inside her mouth.

"Don't worry, Gantsa. Even the best of us come up short sometimes." Cash brushed the cocaine from his fingers. "Let a real nigga show you how to handle this bitch."

Cash was so thirsty and stupid that he didn't even bother with a condom, as he shoved himself roughly inside Purple's juice box and tried to pulverize her, and Kush trying to gag her. She was in a world of pain, and neither of the men seemed to care. With a moan Cash pulled out and squirted off all over Purple's ass, thighs, and calves while Kush continued to fuck her throat.

When she heard Kush's moans become louder, she knew what was about to happen and tried to move her face, but he held her firmly in place by her weave. With a grunt Kush's dick busted in a stream of cum that soaked Purple's face and hair.

"You dirty bitch," Purple cursed him as she wiped cum out of her eyes.

Kush laughed. "My fault, Purple. I couldn't hold it." He dug into his pocket and peeled some money from his bank roll and placed it on the table. "Good looking out. That was some of the meanest head that I ever had. No wonder your nigga ain't left your freaky ass yet."

"What the fuck ever, Kush." Purple picked the bills up and counted them. She looked up at Kush and frowned. "There's only a hundred dollars here, nigga."

"Yeah, you said you wanted a buck to get down," Kush replied.

"I meant a buck apiece, Kush!"

An expression of fake confusion crossed Kush's face. "Oh, I thought you meant a buck for the team. Don't worry, I got you the next time." He tossed Purple her jacket.

"I swear I don't know why I fuck with y'all." Purple stormed toward the door.

"Because money talks and bullshit runs a marathon," Cash taunted her on the way out. Purple slammed the door so hard that the peephole cover was still spinning after she'd gone.

Gantsa laughed. "That bitch was upset as hell."

"Fuck that alcoholic bitch," Kush said, checking a text message that had just come through on his cell phone. "Man, let's roll downstairs so I can meet that nigga King and give him this money." He led them into the hallway and locked the apartment door behind them.

"So what're we getting into after we meet King?" Gantsa asked. After getting his first nut off, he was ready to run a marathon.

"I'm not sure what I'm getting into, but your little ass is gonna play the building and work off that debt you owe. You ain't been on the job but a week or so and you're already fucking up money." Kush shook his head. "That ain't good, dude."

"I know you're mad, Kush, but that nigga ran off with the package. It wasn't my fault," Gantsa tried to explain.

"It is your fault because you should know better than to leave a base head with your dope unattended," Kush scolded him.

"Word up, Gantsa," Cash added.

"And you ain't no fucking better, because I told your stupid ass to hold him down," Kush barked on Cash. "I swear, y'all two muthafuckas is like the blind leading the blind."

The elevator finally came and when it opened, Flash was leaning against the wall in a half nod. When he noticed Kush and his crew standing there, his eyes got as wide as a golf ball.

"Shit!" Flash said, frantically searching for an escape but there was none.

"Shit is right, nigga." Kush snatched him by the front of his coat and yanked him from the elevator. I'm about to show you what we do to thieving crackheads around Thug Town, nigga."

Kush and his crew slapped Flash around and forced him on the rooftop where they stripped him of all his clothes. He stood there, butt ass naked as the day he was born into this world, freezing his ass off, trying to think of a fitting excuse to save his life. Normally, Flash was a wizard with words, but the cold stare Kush was giving him had him at a loss for words. He knew it was a bad idea to rob dealers in the hood where he laid his head, but the monkey that had been clawing at his back had come to bite him on the ass. Flash had fucked up . . . royally.

Kush just stared at him for a long time before finally breaking the silence. "You know you fucked up, right?"

"I know, man, but I'm sure we can work this matter out some kind of way," Flash said, rubbing his arms more out of nervousness than seeking warmth.

"Ain't shit to work out, homey. I don't know you for taking advantage of this lame ass nigga over here—Kush gestured toward Gantsa—because that's what crackheads do, they get over on people. But the fact that you knew it was my dope you still had the nuts to take it is what doesn't sit right with me."

"C'mon, little dude, you know how I get sometimes when I'm sick," he told Gantsa. "Sometimes these drugs make you do stupid things, but I ain't mean no harm. I knew you since you was a little kid." He tried to gain sympathy from Gantsa, but the boy turned away.

"Which only makes it worse," Kush said as he slowly began to circle Flash's trembling form. "If you can rob somebody who you watched grow up, then you is a piece of shit that needs to be dealt with. The only question is: What would make a fitting punishment for what you've done?"

"You know in some countries when you get caught stealing they cut off your hands, nigga," Cash said.

Kush laughed. "What you think, Flash? Should I cut your hands off right now?"

Tears began to run down Flash's ashy face. "Kush, please don't do me like this. Let me work it off."

"These niggas might've been stupid enough to put a package in your hands but I ain't my nigga. We're gonna have to think of something else." Kush scratched his chin and suddenly had a malicious idea. "I've got it, since you flew off with my package let's see if you can fly for real."

"Oh, hell nawl," Flash tried to run, but Cash grabbed him in a chokehold and dragged his bitch ass back.

"Get his legs," Kush ordered Gantsa.

"Huh?" Gantsa asked, shocked.

"Don't huh me, bitch nigga. I said get his legs!" Kush barked.

Gantsa reluctantly approached the squirming Flash to the roof's edge. Kush would change his mind but the taunting look on his face said that it was already a done deal. Gantsa was saddened by the pitiful look in Flash's eyes, but he was frightened by the look in Kush's.

"You got any last words, Flash?" Kush asked.

"Don't do this," Flash pleaded, crying like a baby. Piss ran down his leg and onto Gantsa's hands. It was a disgusting feeling but he was too afraid to let go.

"Toss this bitch!" Kush said.

Flash closed his eyes and said a quick prayer as Cash and Gantsa swayed him back and forth, building momentum, and let him go. "Mama! Mama! Daddy! Daddy!" Flash screamed his throat raw before he realized that he hadn't fallen twenty stories to his death, but only a few to his embarrassment. Instead of throwing him off, they threw him on the ground of the rooftop.

"Flash, do you really think that I would risk a murder charge over a piece of shit like you?" Kush asked.

"Thanks, player. Thank you." Flash wiped his eyes. He was cold, scraped, and pissy but at least he was alive. "Kush, I promise I'll never do anything that stupid again."

"I'm sure you won't." Kush picked up a large brick. "Hold him. Spread-eagle," he told Gantsa and Cash to do. This time they moved without hesitation and stretched Flash's arms out.

"Hold on, you said you weren't gonna kill me." Flash looked up nervously.

"I'm not, but I am going to teach you a lesson," Kush told him before he crushed Flash's right hand with the brick.

***

The instant the bat made contact with the flying baseball, the cracking sound slid through the slider of an opening window and woke her up. Diamond's eyes were barely open when she heard the sound of glass breaking, causing her to jump out of the bed. She ran to the nearest window. Her head was pounding and she felt like she was run over by a loud car. A quick self-pat revealed that a wifebeater was covering her breasts, and her bikini was still intact, an indication that she had not slept with any strangers the night before, but in the past with several females. Instead, the cement-like throb of her scalp meant she had indeed drunk too much alcohol. Her only concern was her house, which had not made contact with the ball. But across the street was old man Beam's brand new Benz. The shiny exterior heightened the fact that there was no longer a back window. The streets were as barren as a desert as he fled from his house and out onto his front porch. He raised his fist and kicked a dirt hole into the perfectly manicured lawn.

She closed the blinds and didn't envy the perpetrators for one moment. She had endured more than a few encounters with the tall, middle-aged widower, mostly when his daughter came home from college during the holidays. His little princess, Ericka, was a borderline nympho but looked as shy as a church mouse. The thought of Ericka drew her back to the pain that had overtaken her head. Diamond dragged herself to the kitchen and pushed open cabinets full of samples from the drug companies. Although she wasn't big on taking medications, she had learned to simply bring home the loaded gift bags she received from pharmaceutical representatives at work.

Her fingers shuffled through the pile and landed on a small box of Tylenol with codeine, but she threw those back in and retrieved some Motrin. Barely able to walk, she opened the refrigerator door and left it wide open. Using the little bit of strength that she was able to muster, she grabbed the orange juice container and gulped down four, maybe six, pills.

It took every moment of the long and excruciating twenty-two minutes before her hand could move without the thrust of pool balls bashing against her skull. She headed for the shower, and the streams of water against her face and chest felt soothing. Her hands ran down her chest and she cupped her breasts while her other hand slid between her thighs. Barely grazing her clit, she shivered and tucked her middle finger deep inside her pussy. With each thrust her nipples grew harder, resurrecting in her mind the feel of Ericka's body wrapped around her own physique.

Initially, the daydream was laced with the soft flesh of Ericka's medium-sized breasts nestled against her back, as Little Miss Princess pasted electrified kisses all along her neck and shoulder. What really drove Diamond crazy was the sensation of Ericka's pubic hairs rubbing against her behind while her hands gently kneaded her belly and thighs. Ericka always liked the role of being teased, so Diamond would grab her hands and spin her around so they could make eye-to-eye contact.

Just then, Diamond was snatched out of wishful thinking and back into the throes of reality, by the sound of someone knocking at the front door. She slammed her hands against the wall, mumbling unrecognizable obscenities under her breath. She wrapped the towel around her curvaceous body and put on a thin robe. Every two steps were met with a slightly less intense clash inside her skull. Soon the repercussions of overdrinking would subside, or so she hoped. She struggled to look through the peephole.

Intending to yell, she barely squeaked out, "Who is it at the door?"

His voice sounded more like a plea than his usual command. "It's Beam."

She opened the front door. "Come on in." Diamond cracked a slight smile and waved in a welcoming way. Mr. Beam didn't look at her but marched directly into her house like an invited guest.

"Did you hear that loud noise outside?" he asked.

She could see where Ericka got her chiseled facial bone structure and the slightly Asian-looking eyes.

"Nawl, I mean yeah, I heard something a bit ago . . .but I was asleep. It woke me up."

Mr. Beam was sitting on the couch by then, moving the "Consequence of the Game" book to the side that should have been in the bedroom. This book was written by Tony Daniels, a great author that wrote a children's book called *Bounce Bunny and Friends.*

"Ah, well, they hit my car."

The expression on his face startled her. He had always seemed tough and brash but appeared vulnerable at the moment.

"By the time I got to the window no one was on the street."

"Sorry about your car," she added. She tried to reflect sympathy in her voice but the hangover still pounded through her head. He scanned the contents of the house, glanced at the door and then seemed to be peeking into the kitchen, like he was searching for something in particular.

"You've got a nice crib."

"Thanks."

Mr. Beam looked at the Chanel robe she was wearing and then placed the magazines back in their original place on the coffee table, like he was trying to help her organize.

Rising to stand, his stature seemed almost too muscular for a man his age. "I just came by to find out if you saw anything."

She shook her head as he turned to let himself out the front door. "I bet it was probably some damn kids." He took one last look around and slammed the door behind him.

She had moved into the Pear Tree Heights neighborhood about six years prior, when she had started medical school. The house had been empty for a few years, since the death of her daddy. Her grandfather, his beneficiary, didn't have the heart to sell it. She offered to rent the crib out and her people offered to buy it. But, to the surprise of everyone, her grandfather surprised her and signed over the deed. He had always seemed distant and emotionally detached from her but insisted that it was a gift for graduating from college and undertaking medical school.

Pear Tree Heights was a middle-to-upper-class community comprised mostly of blacks and located near the Mississippi County Community College. Diamond had grown up in the heart of Blytheville, Arkansas and the University town contrasted greatly from the inner city. Unlike where she had grown up, it was substantially harder to find a liquor store; not that she needed them.

Liquor stores were few and far between and, unlike an inner city, were nestled in some unsuspecting places on the outskirts of town. Also, mostly everything closed around eight, with the exception of the posh restaurants and small theaters. The town was centered around the campus and felt abandoned in the summer but overpopulated during the regular school year.

Diamond had been in medical school and living in the house for a few months before she finally decided to attend her first club party. Upon leaving her house, she closed up the garage door and decided to ride her red motorcycle, a sparkling GT 750 Ducati. But before she could start the engine, a woman ran toward her and yelled, "Those wheels are nice. I thought you were a guy for a second but it's all good."

Ericka sashayed around the motorcycle, staring straight into Diamond's eyes. She stood about five-four and disguised her slim figure with a large, shiny, patent-leather black belt that complemented her blue chiffon blouse and straight Khaki shirt. But what truly caught Diamond's attention were her green bedroom eyes. They looked sexy against her perfect, milk-dark, smooth skin and her brown, wavy hair with auburn highlights.

"Can a bitch go for a ride?" Her smile was confident and Diamond wondered if she knew what she was doing at the moment.

Diamond laughed, put her hand out, and introduced herself. When Ericka held her hand longer than usual, it was clear she knew exactly what she was doing but Diamond couldn't push past her church girl exterior. She declined to take Ericka on a ride and was met with a long face.

Ericka pointed to the house directly across the street, indicating that it was where she lived. Ericka was a straight, no-chaser kind of girl, so she pulled a pen from her pocket and wrote her phone number inside the palm of Diamond's hand. Diamond played it cool and a kiss was planted on Diamond's cheek and, within seconds, Ericka turned and switched her small hip as she strutted toward her crib.

Diamond revved her motor and glided at a slow pace out of her driveway, then stopped in front of the curb where Ericka now stood. She flipped up the visor on her helmet and winked at Ericka.

Ericka looked her up and down as she licked her full lips and puckered them, feigning a kiss. Before Diamond could settle into the tingling between her legs, her eyes couldn't help but focus on the face of an angry man standing at the front door. Diamond was nobody's fool and recognized the territorial protective look of a man who was either her father, or boyfriend. Diamond cranked the engine full throttle and sped off.

Diamond left the party early. Her first thought was to call Ericka but the thought of the old man followed behind her. Diamond coasted into her driveway. The neighborhood was dead quiet and the house across the street was completely dark. Just as Diamond was opening her door, there was a slight tap on her shoulder. Startled, she jumped and nearly fell off the small porch. Ericka jumped back in response but caught the falling Diamond.

With a slight chuckle, she said, "I'm sorry. I didn't mean to scare you."

Diamond composed herself and started to laugh from the pit of her stomach. Ericka joined in and the two wiped away tears that resulted from the long laughter. Diamond fumbled with her keys and the moment the door was closed, the two locked lips like pitbulls. Ericka slithered her tongue from Diamond's earlobe to her clothed nipples.

Her gaze caught Diamond's eyes rolling to the back of her head as her body went limp. The two unfastened, unzipped, and unbuttoned at the speed of lightning until they were completely nude. Diamond wrapped her small hands around Ericka's firm behind and hoisted her up around her waist. Ericka became the damsel in distress as Diamond smothered her face within Ericka's chest and carried her upstairs to the bedroom.

The snake-like motion of Ericka's tongue landed between Diamond's thighs. The flickering sensation got a rise out of her clit, which grew rounder and firmer. Ericka's tongue lashing intensified as she lapped up every last drop of moisture from the head of her mound to the eyelet of her anus. Diamond's back arched, pushing every bit of being onto Ericka's face.

"You like that, don't you?" Ericka said as she pulled Diamond's hips tighter and tighter.

"Fuck me," Diamond whispered, hoping it was just a thought and not audible words. But when Ericka's fingers penetrated with a rhythmic motion while her mouth gently suctioned the flesh of her chubby clit, Diamond suspended disbelief and released an orgasm that nearly drowned Ericka's face and hands.

"That's right, babe. Give it, honey. That's what a bitch needs and is here for. Yeah, I like that."

Diamond felt a sense of comfort and frustration. She attempted to pull away from Ericka but her grip was locked and her hand was nearly fully inside. This would be the first time Diamond had let a woman fist her and with each circular motion, she experienced her pussy walls receiving the small, balled hand of her new lover. Her orgasm subsided with spikes of energy driving her nearer and nearer to the next moment of ecstasy.

Screaming at a pitch she thought was only capable of girly girls, Diamond was shocked at the explosion of excitement she felt in every cell of her body, including the edges of her finger-tips. Ericka's hand was nestled deep inside her womanhood as orgasmic rays pulsated through her body and provoked miniature convulsions. Sweat poured from her flesh like running water. They were both surprised when a jetstream of cum peaked at a height of about two to three feet.

"Dayum, baby. I didn't know you were a squirter."

Ericka leaned back to enjoy the sight, and Diamond was slightly embarrassed but too excited to let it show.

Diamond's body lay flat and lifeless. Ericka brought a warm washcloth from the bathroom and patted the sweat from Diamond's forehead and neck. Their eyes met again;

they searched for more answers, hoping to define their connection. Diamond lied about leaving the party or even going to it, as you can see. Diamond smiled at the stranger and started to wonder when the sunlight would vanish from their interaction, but then stopped herself. This time she would not go there; this time she would enjoy it with an ounce and half of hope.

Ericka finished drying off the rest of Diamond's body and lay next to her. Diamond's muscular arms drew her closer as the two held each other. Before the sound of morning birds, the two had tossed the sheets of sexual bliss several more times.

Diamond caught a nap before she had to go to the medical school and woke to an empty bed with a small note that read:

"We must do this again and again and again."

A generous smile swept her face and a steady throb evolved within her pussy.

Chapter 7

Junebug eased his Benz into the vacant warehouse lot. He'd been sulking and snooting for the last hour as he sipped Remy in silence. Only mumbling a few phrases to himself.

"Junebug baby, what are we going here?" asked a nervous Candice. Despite the numerous questions, he remained quiet, only checking his Rolex periodically. Junebug answered with more silence, giving a look of determination and murder before he got out of the coupé. He walked into the building containing the climate-controlled storage units. Candice had to almost jog to keep up when he finally stopped at a single unit with the number 21-B above it. He quickly unlocked it and dragged Candice inside. When he hit the light, Candice lost her breath instantly. Inside were five large gun safes of various shades of black, gray, and green. That was nothing. What took her breath was the stacked olive drab queen coats stenciled with the United States Army in pale yellow. Junebug immediately opened two of the five safes and pulled out two military grade M-4s, handing one to her. He strapped on two leg holsters, then grabbed a matching FN-5-7'x, checked for loads, and slipped them into the holsters.

Junebug was a man possessed, knowing what was to come. He furiously threw fully automatic Glock 18 drums and extra ammo into two large black duffle bags. Candice had yet to move, being more than impressed by the well-stocked arsenal. Just as well she knew a lot of people were about to die.

"Junebug, you can't do this. I know you're upset, baby."

He turned to face her so fast, so aggressively she staggered.

"Don't call me *baby*, or tell me what I can't do. I lost my soulmate and my fucking cousin. For all I care you can fucking go, bitch," snapped Junebug as he placed four hand grenades in one of the duffle bags. Standing on her tiptoes, she placed a warm kiss on the back of his neck before she rested her head on his back.

"Baby, I'm with you till the end. Stop fighting me."

Junebug turned to face her, then stared into her beautiful eyes. "Why?"

"Because I know your pain. Someone murdered my father. Anyone would feel this way. My mother died giving birth to me. I have nobody but my gun, job, and my sex toys." Embarrassed and vulnerable, Candice giggled and dropped a lone tear. "My heart has found a place with you. If you want me I'm yours. Regardless of you being in the streets, you're a man, a leader, true to your love like my father. I need you, Junebug."

That's when the dam broke. Candice cried uncontrollably into Junebug's chest, and at that very moment Junebug knew he was going to give her whatever she asked for. He was officially hers. That's when his tears came falling down. For even though he had yet to bury his family, he had just put them to rest in his heart. He knew Carla would want him happy, and out of the game.

She'd want him to have a good woman who was her equal, or better just as Candice was. Junebug's life would go on because they would live through him. Giving in, he kissed her full lips and caressed her back downwards, with his hands resting on her ass. Instantly his dick hardened just as she became wet. They both were ready until they heard noise from outside which altered their moment of elation. The sound of shuffling, and an audible "Shhh" caused them to be alert.

Junebug checked his watch, then immediately went into action. He tossed Candice a level 3 flak vest that she put on, then he put on his own quickly. She dove into the first safe and grabbed a fully automatic MP-5 and tossed a few mags into a bag. Finished, Junebug grabbed an RPG and a coat, and slung it over his shoulder onto his back.

"Junebug, now what, nigga? We can't go out there, it could be an ambush, we're pinned!" Candice said, shouldering the smallest bag. In response he smirked.

"Would I be that nigga if I didn't plan this?" He then opened the fourth safe and popped a panel out to reveal a tunnel. "Come on. Just stay to the right."

"How'd you know they'd come?" she asked, impressed. Candice clicked on the flashlight on the MP-5 submachine and stepped in. Junebug had yet to enter when she called for him. Junebug pressed a series of buttons on the pad of the 5th safe and hurriedly followed Candice. After a brisk minute they came to a dead end when Junebug removed a hidden panel. The tunnel led them to another storage that contained a satin black Benz G-63 truck. Reaching under the front wheel, he produced the keys. Tossing the bags in, he directed Candice to get in the driver's seat.

"I'm going to open the door—don't go out till I signal you," he instructed.

"Junebug, that's a stupid plan. Let's go out on foot first, and take out as many as we can. I've got the training, trust me!" Candice said defiantly.

Relenting, Junebug shrugged and stepped out of her way. As they stepped out into the night, the moon graced them with enough light to see that the Bentley was blocked in by a van. There were about 6-8 men standing around, and an untold number inside. "I see about eight with small arms. Unknown numbers inside, they could have found the tunnel by now."

He smirked yet again.

"Nah, they didn't find it yet," he stated as an explosion rocked them, causing Candice to duck and Junebug to laugh. "Now they found it." Apparently he rigged it to blow. Those standing outside were now disoriented. That's when Candice's true training kicked in. Unexpectedly, she stepped out with Junebug on her heels.

She clicked off the safety and fired at the first of three men, delivering double-tap center mass shots to each at a distance of 30 yards.

The remaining five scrambled for safety. That's when she flicked to full auto. Candice sent 9mm rounds into the back of two of them, landing 90% of the shots fired. Junebug, not hesitating, squeezed his M4 and managed to hit one man and sprayed the Bentley by accident. He had enough money, and actually cared little about losing the expensive car. But a woman had the training to handle a fully automatic so skillfully. Then the last two men fired from behind the bullet-proof Bentley. Candice returned fire while Junebug pulled the pin and tossed a grenade, rolling it under the Bentley. When the car exploded, Junebug shielded Candice as it set off a chain reaction. The van exploded, sending parts of it and the coupé raining down across the lot. Once it slowed down, Junebug stood in time to see a black Charger speed off, knowing one of Moe's men escaped, and the police were on the way as they raced back to the Benz truck. Junebug took the wheel and it started with a deep growl. He smashed the gas pedal and pushed it out of the storage units quickly. Junebug took pride in everything he did, so it showed in the upgrades he did on this monster. Bullet proofing, upgrade engine, crash bars, and electronics. It even had internal satellite TVs and a refrigerator. It also had guns installed in the front and back.

"Baby, where are we going?" Candice asked Junebug as they merged onto the freeway. With the look of the devil, he answered his own question.

"How did you learn to shoot like that? I've seen police, feds, shoot and that ain't it. No more lies, Candice."

The truth was out, thought Candice.

"I trained with the FEDS, and did a four-year tour with a terrorist unit in Baghdad away."

Junebug smiled at her. Candice had so many layers, how could he not fall for her?

"What? Why are you smiling? It's not funny!" said Candice, clearly upset.

"Nah, you complement me. But I knew something was up with   you."

She returned his smile and playfully slapped his arm. She thought to herself that he didn't know the half of it as he pushed the Benz to 100 mph.

Just outside of the city, Junebug pushed the big body Benz 465 horse-powered engine to its limits. Racing to Moe's mansion, his intent was to murder him and whoever stood between them. Junebug hadn't spoken a word, giving Candice the opportunity to use Google maps to study the layout of the property. Before she could finish, Junebug pulled into the parking lot, and began checking his weapons. He downsized one of his bags and was prepared to go in as if he were Rambo. Candice knew that if they did, it would be bloodshed on both sides. She attempted to put a stop to him.

"Junebug, we can't go in like a movie scene, or we may never make it out," Candice said, causing Junebug to stare at her.

"Trust me, babe, Moe is the bigger fish, not his nephew Fresh. We can't die before we make it to him."

"What do you suggest, Mayor?" Junebug said sarcastically.

"Fuck you!" Candice snapped, popping her lips.

"Nawl, fuck with me," he joked.

"I promised I'll take all that dick if we walk away from this."

"You got it, now what's up?"

Candice smiled and kissed Junebug's lip before she pointed across the street. "Go to that auto parts store on Main Street." Doing as he was told, he drove her to the store. She entered the store, and re-emerged minutes later eating a pack of skittles she purchased at the counter.

"I know you ain't stop me for a bag of skittles?"

"Nope," replied Candice. She then opened the bag, revealing a small spool of wire, a battery-operated drill, two spark plugs, electrical tape and a pair of wire cutters. Junebug looked confused.

"I don't even want to know, do I?"

Candice shook her head and smirked. "Nah, now take me to a local gas station.

***

Moe yelled out in anger, despite feeling the sudden doubt and fear of Junebug's wrath coming on. The remaining men he had were a little shook themselves, but hung around due to the promise of the million in cash they'd get if they killed Junebug.

"You muthafuckers get in postion! I'll personally kill your family if Junebug gets away again!" At that very moment the sounds of a breaking window on the ground floor disrupted his threats. Moe paused, waiting to hear anything else. That's when a small explosion rocked the mansion. Moe snatched up his Mack 90 and barked at his men. "Go! Go! No one makes it near me! Kill everything that moves!" The men, snapping to, followed orders and filed out of the room into the hallways. Just then, a second explosion went off beneath his balcony. This one sent a massive jolt through the house. The last man through the door lost his footing and hit Biscuit in the head. The other three desperately ducked as Glizzy's body stiffened, causing him to squeeze the trigger on his janky ass TEC- 9. The fully automatic weapon fired, spraying shots into the carpeted floors, sending white tufts into the air in a line. The trail of bullets and damage reached two of the middle guys, hitting them in the legs, stomach, and chest. Neither were dead, just incapacitated and worthless. The so-called shooters lost their cockiness, and the once well regarded prestige they held of being called killers. This left Moe with himself and two men. As the realization hit him, he knew he might die right at this very moment. Pride and arrogance fueled him and he considered it: it was only Junebug and some bitch against him and two shooters. His office was set up just like Scarface's was in the movie. He had security monitors all across the wall so he could see from the front. An automatic Russian military special, an AK-47, was in his gun safe. The gun had a 100-round drum, and a grenade launcher on the bottom.

He moved out into the hallway, remembering Fresh's warning. Fresh had claimed to have seen the assassin bitch shoot and kill six men with ease, barely missing. The shit had happened a while back. But the memory of it made Moe reconsider his options. He decided to escape. "Get me to the garage!" Leaving the wounded men, they surrounded Moe and cautiously made their way through the hot smoke-filled mansion. He expected that Junebug had made it into the crib by now. Yet they made it to the garage without issue. There Moe had his choice of five cars to escape in, but only one was bullet-proof. The Yukon Denali was decked with run flats, bullet-proof glass doors, and panels. Moe instantly felt safer as he grinned a silent victory.

Junebug threw the third grenade that was taped to a gas can. Then he ran to Candice at the mansion's long driveway. They reached the Benz at the same time.

"You really think he's going to go for it? He can't be that crazy," Junebug said as he caught his breath. Candice looked into his brown eyes as she responded.

"Play the odds, babe. We took North, East, and South, leaving the only exit being West, the garage. Plus, he strikes me as the cowardly type!" she said, leaning towards Junebug, looking in his eyes.

"Leaving it up to you, unh?" he asked sarcastically. She was inches from his face when they finally kissed. Their lips locked as hungry tongues met in the middle. Candice released her MP-5, and grabbed his large dick through his pants. Things were getting hot and heavy when the fourth explosion sent debris raining down over them. Candice tensed, anticipating it and giggling as it stopped.

"Pardon my language, but you're a sick bitch," said Junebug as he stood. He then gave her his hand and helped her up. She twisted her face up in protest at the word *bitch*. "But you're cute and sexy as hell."

"Shut up and go finish this nigga," she replied, shaking the dirt and rocks from her hair. Junebug pulled the RPG from the bag and headed to finish off Moe.

Chapter 8

The sounds of "Hummingbird," Keith Sweat's song, played softly on the portable CD player while Ebony sat on her tattered living room couch, staring out the front window at the twinkling lights of the projects. She was going to bust out the Wii Fit game and do some yoga, but she was drained so she decided to sip some hot tea and sort through the old mail she'd found in the kitchen drawer.

"Bills, bills, bills," Ebony muttered as she tossed the envelopes into the trash can one at a time. Halfway through the pile, she came across an envelope addressed to her from the State of Arkansas. It was a letter from the welfare office notifying her that she had to come in for recertification or risk benefits being cut off. The deadline for her to come in had been two days prior, which explained while her EBT card no longer worked. She knew that she hadn't gotten the letter out of the mailbox, which meant it had to be Tony's handiwork. Just thinking about all the drama she would have to go through to recertify sent her pressure through the roof, and she was about to give Tony's little ass hell.

Tony almost jumped out of his black skin when she stormed into his bedroom unannounced. He was lying across the bed with his hand in his pants and watching something on his laptop that didn't want his mother to see.

"Don't you know how to knock before you come in?" Tony asked, flipping the screen closed.

"I pay the bills in this bitch. I don't have to do shit to come straight in your room. Tony, when did this letter come?" She tossed the letter across the bed.

"I don't remember. I opened it and put it back inside the mailbox."

"What the hell do you mean, you don't know? You got it out of the mailbox, didn't you?"

"Yeah," he shrugged and went about the task of loading Madden NFL 2024. She stopped between him and the television, blocking his view. "What's your problem?"

"My problem is that your irresponsible ass got our food stamps cut off because you didn't give me this letter. Now I gotta go to the welfare and sort all this shit out tomorrow."

Tony looked at her quizzically. "So what's the big deal? You should be a pro at this by now."

She reached down and ripped the wires from the game.

He bolted upright. "Chill out before you break my game!"

"You don't buy shit around here. Your attitude has been really twisted lately and I dislike it."

"I don't got no attitude. You the one acting like a crazy mother in front of my friends all the time." He folded his arms.

"Who? That degenerate ass Kush? Boy, you can't be serious. And you know damn well that the reason I went in is because I told you not to be posted up in front of the building with Kush, Cash, and Junebug."

"I wasn't chilling with them. I was with Gantsa.

She laughed. "As if his ass is still innocent, little nigga. I don't understand why you and Gantsa can't just hang out here and play video games like y'all used to instead of getting caught up in these projects."

"Mom, you can only play video games for so long. Nobody wants to be stuck in the house all day long. You don't let me go outside the hood, and when I go in front of the project to get some fresh air you scream at me. I can't win at all."

She took a long deep breath and sat on the edge of his bed. "Tony, why can't you understand that I'm trying to keep you out of harm's way? Every time you turn around, somebody is either getting locked up in jail or killed in a drug war around here in these streets. You cannot turn on the news these days without seeing a grieving parent. A mother's nightmare is losing her child to this bullshit and I'm trying to make sure you're safe, son, that's all."

He sat up and folded his arms again. "Come on, mom, I know what time it is on the streets. That's why I don't mess around with the stuff Kush and these niggas are into. Just because you may see me with them doesn't mean I'm out there doing what they do."

"That may be true, Tony, but the police aren't gonna care. If they swoop down on you, it won't matter if they're Kush's, Gantsa's, or your drugs, the police will divide them among the three of you and take all of your asses to the police station."

"Not me, mom. If the police roll on the block, I'm getting outta there quick," Tony said as if he had it all figured out.

"Son, are you out of your damn mind? Don't even run from the police, all that will do is give them a reason to shoot you."

Tony waved her off. "You don't know what's up out there."

"Little boy, I've probably forgotten more than you will ever learn. I became pregnant when I was only a few years older than you are now. I was already pregnant when I found out I was carrying you. And after I gave birth, I've always been the rock that holds this family together, so you can't tell me anything about knowing what's up out there. It's you who hasn't got a clue. Tony, you can barely wipe your ass let alone survive out on your own. Stop being a smart ass and listen to what I'm saying to you."

"Okay, mom." He went back to his video game.

She stared at him for a long period of time and said nothing. She could see that same determined look in his eyes that Ted had whenever he was plotting, and this is what scared her the most. She had bent over backward to raise her son right. Despite her efforts as a mother, she realized she couldn't fully prepare him for the world as a man. It was times like those when she wished that she had someone in her life to provide a positive example of manhood for him, but she didn't, so until the situation changed she would have to wear both pairs of pants. She got up off the bed and headed towards the door. "Tony, the leftovers from dinner are in the microwave. I've got my key so don't go to the door for anyone while I'm gone."

"Where are you going, mom?" he asked, as if he were her boyfriend or paid bills in the house.

"Out for a minute," she said over her shoulder before slamming the bedroom door. She welcomed the cool air that ran across her face when she came out of the building. She loved the tranquility of her cozy little apartment but sometimes it felt like the walls were closing in on her, especially when she was having problems with her son, which seemed to be more and more frequent the older he got. Sometimes he stressed her out so bad that she wanted to put her foot in his ass, but the guilt she carried for the fact that he was growing up fatherless stayed her anger.

Tony, like most young children, didn't ask to be in this world, but God made a way for him anyhow. As parents they had a moral obligation to the children but not everyone held up their end of the bargain, which was the case with Ted. When things got bad in the house she sometimes questioned her decision to have a child so young, but every time she looked at him the doubt evaporated. She loved Tony more than anything and will go above and beyond to protect him, which is what Kush and his little crew needed to get into their ignorant little brains. Just breathe, she told herself. She took stock of her surroundings and realized that she had walked all the way across town. She was not only aggravated and confused, but almost a half mile away from the apartment she was in no rush to get back to. For as much as she loved Tony, she couldn't deal with him at that moment. She spent all of her time taking care of him and that night she wanted to be taken care of. After digging a quarter out of her pocket, she found a local pay phone boost and dialed Smoke's phone number.

Tony gave his mother about ten minutes before he slipped into his Tom Ford jacket and headed for the front door. He stopped in front of the mirror to give himself the once-over before slipping out the door. He knew his mother would try and kill him if she found out that he'd gone out after dark, which was why he had no intentions of getting caught. By the time he made it out the door into the elevator to the lobby door, his whole demeanor had changed. His happy schoolboy jaunt slowed to a hop and a scowl melted over his face. The drop in the temperature had sent most people indoors, but the few who made their lives in the courtyard remained. Nodding to a few heads he knew, Tony walked from the front of apartments over to the bench where Cash and Gantsa were applying their trade.

"Oh, shit, my nigga." Cash ribbed him as soon as he walked up. He was sitting on the backseat of the bench, passing something to an older guy that Tony had seen around before.

"What's good, nigga?" Tony gave Cash dap and then his best friend Gantsa dap.

"Tony, your mother is gonna flip out if she catches you out here." Gantsa looked around nervously as if she would spring from the bushes at any moment.

"Nah, she gone for a minute or two." He took a seat on the bench next to Gantsa. "What's good with y'all fools?"

"Out here chasing a dollar or two. Fuck is good with you?" Cash asked in an accusatory tone as he twisted a long Cuban cigar back and forth between his fingers.

"You know how I keep it," Tony said in a hip tone that made Cash scoff.

"Yeah, which is why I'm trying to figure out what you're doing out here after the street lights have come on?"

"Come on, player, stop trying to play me like I'm one of the little niggas from behind the center or something," Tony said. It always irritated him when the older heads made fun of his mother's tight yoke on him, but Cash especially.

"Don't be fooled, Cash is just playing," Gantsa said in an attempt to ease the discomfort he knew his friend was feeling.

Cash just scoffed and proceeded to split the cigar down the middle.

"So, where'd your mother go to have you feeling frog enough to be out here handing with the scumbags?"

"I don't really know." Tony shrugged. She broke out on some fake mad shit a while ago. She's probably up the block at Keisha's crib."

"Hey, that is one bad hood bitch!" Gantsa said excitedly.

"Yeah and she's out of your league, little stud," Cash said, shooting him down.

"The way I hear it she's outta anybody's league unless it's Sam's," Tony added his three cents.

"See," Cash began as he lit the blunt he'd expertly rolled, "that's the problem with y'all players. You always got your mouth in grown people business and don't know what you're talking about."

"Man, everybody knows Keisha is Sam's baby mother and the nigga is straight up crazy over her," Gantsa said.

"That ain't the word on the block. Sam got a bitch on the westside that he's claiming as his wife so Keisha is up for the highest bidder. My nigga Kush sizing that up for a minute." Cash handed the loud blunt to Gantsa. The boy tried to hit the blunt like a champion and damn near choked to death.

Tony looked at Cash quizzically. "Keisha is a serious ass broad and only fucks with boss niggas. If anything I'd think she'd be trying to set it out to King, if anybody."

"King ain't the boss of shit!" Cash said sharply. "All that nigga does is go between us and the man holding the yay. Tony, you see for yourself every time you come out here it's us on the money. This hood and all the money that passes through it belongs to us. You better ask your homie, shorty stuff."

"He ain't lying," Gantsa said and pulled a knot of money out of his pocket to prove it. "We be getting stupid money outta here in these apartments, Tony." He waved the cash proudly. The wad was money from the drug package, not Gantsa's, but Tony was naive enough to be enticed.

Gantsa laughed. "Relax, it's only some green. "What, you think we gonna give you Angel Dust or something on the sneak side to harm you?" He tried to loosen him up but Tony was still hesitant at the moment. "Gantsa, I told you this young nigga was a square from the start."

Tony sat on the bench feeling like every set of eyes in the entire project were focused on him. In the back of his mind he could hear his mother giving him a speech about gateway drugs, but it was drowned out by the mocking stare he was getting from Cash and his desire to belong. "Fuck it," Tony said and snatched the weed.

Chapter 9

Ebony wasn't sure how it had happened but ended up at Smoke's crib. She had called him just to shoot the breeze on the payphone and try to burn off some steam before she went back home where her son at. The more she talked, the more she opened up about what was going on with her. The next thing she knew she was crying and Smoke was pulling up to the corner in his Range Rover. They rode around for a minute and talked a while sipping Moët and smoking several Purple Kush blunts. She hadn't even realized that they'd left so fast until he was parking the truck on a nice block. It was a tastefully decorated studio with severe big screen televisions and a futon. He'd claimed he only needed seven minutes to grab his Gucci wallet and change his jacket. That seven minutes turned into more. They ended up watching a movie and touching each other's hair on their head.

Ebony was at peace, lying across the futon, watching the movie, and it reminded her of her uncle in federal prison. She didn't get this kind of solitude with Tony's aunties and staring at the drab yellow walls of her apartment. Without even realizing what she had done, she snuggled closer to him.

"Ebony, a nigga missed this part of holding you."

"Ah, ah!"

"No, this." He motioned to them. "Remember when we used to do this all the time together, lay around and watch movies?"

"Yeah, it would be nice until your cell phone starts ringing and you'd head to the bathroom to take the call." Ebony sat up straight in the bed. "Smoke, I didn't really come over here to go down memory lane with you. I have enough negative stuff running around in my head already without adding our failed romance to it."

"Babe, how can you call something that was never given a chance to work *failed*? When things were good between us they were good. Don't you miss it at all?"

"Yeah, I do," she admitted, "but I'm not willing to pay the price bag you're trying to hang on it. Yo, men continued to baffle me with the way they move. Y'all can have something that's priceless and you still want more. Why can't you ever be satisfied with just one piece of pussy?"

"Because we're greedy," he said honestly. "Now before you go all crazy on me, let me explain. Men, we're like animals, meaning we move off instinct instead of thoughts. No matter how much a nigga loves his woman, he's always gonna lust after other women, it's just how we're wired. But this doesn't mean we always gonna act on it. Our base desire is to conquer women . . . it's so hard to be faithful, but it's not impossible to be with one woman."

"Then why did you make it seem so impossible?" she asked.

"Because back then I didn't have that kind of discipline like now." He gave her a sincere look. The seriousness she saw behind his eyes caused her to turn away but he made her look at him. "I'm a different man now, babe." He placed a kiss on her lips off guard softly and ran his hand down her sexy body.

"Smoke, don't." She pulled away, but it was half-hearted. It had been so long since she had been touched by a man that it felt almost electric. She wanted to give herself to him, but she was afraid at the moment.

"Ebony, you don't have to carry your burdens around anymore." He kissed her again and this time she kissed him back. "Let me help you carry them, baby, around." He smiled.

Time wrapped in on itself, blurring the lines between seconds, minutes, and even hours. It felt like Smoke had one thousand hands as he seemed to touch her body everywhere at once, lighting small fires under her beautiful skin and deep in her gut. She floated down onto the futon and let him command her body. He slipped between her legs, kissing her neck and stomach while he worked her pussy moist with two fingers. His dick felt heavy in his hand when he pulled it out and tried to glide it inside her pussy. He had almost penetrated her when she stopped him in his tracks.

"I know you got a condom?" he pleaded, feeling like he was going to cum prematurely. He couldn't believe he asked her a stupid question like that.

"I'm already feeling like this is a big mistake, so if I were you I'd wrap this monster before I change my mind." She reached down and stroked his thick dick fast motion, dripping pre-cum onto her thick thighs.

He grumbled something and rolled off her and walked toward the bathroom with his dick rock-hard slapping against his thighs. A few seconds later he came back into the bedroom with a *Magnum* rubber package for her approval.

"That's more like it," she said with a smile.

He rolled the condom over his throbbing manhood and lowered himself on top of her again. She was tight, so tight that even with her own moisture and the lubricant from the condom he couldn't get it in without hurting both of them. He parted her legs and lowered his face to her pussy where he proceeded to work his tongue inside her, sending jolts of pleasure through her limbs. She dragged her nails across the back of his scalp while he worked her to a nice lather. She stared up at the ceiling as spots danced before her eyes while he continued to punish her pussy. She was taking his dick like a real pro. Her heart screamed "no," but her body barked "yes," and she tried to shove his whole face inside her. All of her fears and apprehensions faded away, leaving only the longing to feel him inside her and she let him know by reluctantly pulling his face free of her wet pussy.

His goatee was slick with her pussy juices, as he looked down into her hungry eyes. He knew just what she wanted and intended to give it to her. Now that she was wet enough it was a little easier to enter her. He slipped a little of his dick into her tight pussy, silently calling on God and every other saint he could think of. Her pussy was like a beam of sunshine shining down on his face on a hot day. With every stroke inside her pussy he could feel her walls tighten around his hard dick, making him want to go deeper than the ocean. He held out for twenty minutes before the buildup became too much for him and he exploded inside the condom like a rocket ship into space. He continued pumping and humping like a dog as the cum kept pouring from his dick, eventually spilling out over the rim of the condom and dripping onto the futon. When he felt the last of it and his strength faded, he collapsed on top of her, sucking his thumb like a baby.

"Nigga, you tryin' to kill me. I'm not a young thot anymore." She laughed in a joking manner, but was telling the truth.

"King Kong don't have nothing on me right now!"

***

By the time Tony rolled out of bed, his mother was already dressed and had breakfast on the table, which he thought was strange since they were both notoriously dysfunctional in the mornings and hated waking up. What he didn't know was that she had never gone to sleep since leaving Smoke's house. She'd prepared a hearty meal of pancakes, eggs, and of course turkey sausage. Her parents had never fed their kids pork and she never gave it to her son.

"What's up with you this morning, mom?" he asked her as she was washing dishes and cooking breakfast at the same time but a different way this morning.

"What do you mean, son?" she asked, doing the two steps in front of the sink.

"I mean why are you so happy? You've been floating around this kitchen like Megan Thee Stallion or somebody all morning."

"Boy, you're tripping, I'm just in a good mood. Life ain't all about being sour," she said, drying her hands on the dish towel.

Tony placed his hand on her forehead. "You sure you not sick or something?"

"Boy, get outta here and get your coat and bag so you can catch the bus and I can go handle my business about my food stamps." She shooed him.

While Tony went off to get his school things, she took a few minutes to reflect on her evening with Smoke. The first round was the bomb, but a little uncomfortable because it had been so long for her, but rounds two and three were out of this world. She and Smoke had gone at it until the wee hours of the morning before he finally took her home so that she would be there to get Tony ready for school. Part of her felt guilty for backsliding and letting Smoke hit it and reopening the door for his bullshit, but she promised herself she wouldn't get caught up this time. For as much as she was feeling Smoke, she knew she had to play the situation between them just like it was: friends with benefits. As long as she didn't let her emotions get involved, she'd be okay, or at least she hoped as much.

"You ready?" He came into the kitchen startling her.

"Oh, yeah, let's go." She grabbed her Chanel bag and her coat.

"Are you sure you're okay, mom?"

She paused for a minute, then smiled. "Sure am, son. In fact, I haven't felt this good in a while. Now let's go catch your bus."

She put Tony on his bus ten minutes later. She headed over to the bus station so she could get to see her case worker about her food stamps. From past experience she knew that calling wouldn't do much more than upset her, so she decided to deal with the matter in person. She arrived at the welfare building at 9:30 a.m. and could already tell that the day was gonna be one big headache. She got there early to beat the crowd only to find that there was some kind of staff meeting so the appointment was delayed by an hour. She had to fight through a throng of rude security guards, loud women, and whining babies before she was finally able to speak to someone and tell her what she was there for.

The woman behind the desk seemed to have a nasty attitude when she flung the stack of paperwork across the table to her and ordered her to take a seat until her name was called. Her first reaction was to curse the woman out but that would only delay the process, so she just took the paperwork and went to find a chair somewhere.

The waiting was filled almost to capacity with men, women, and children who all seemed to have an issue.

She managed to find a seat in the corner near the window and went to the task of filling out the papers. The process was even more irritating than the first time she'd gone through it, with the million and one questions they asked you on the forms. Some of the information wasn't even necessary; it was just the state trying to get in your business.

Halfway through the paperwork she found her space invaded as two young kids ran past her, coming close enough to almost step on her foot. Bringing up the rear was a girl who couldn't have been more than twenty-two-years old if she was a day over. Her short hair was hastily slicked into a greasy ponytail and held in place by a child's pop bow. She looked from the stroller the girl was pushing to the bulge under her shirt and shook her head. She was just one of many little girls who were trying to grow up too fast around this bitch.

"Anybody sitting there?" the girl asked Ebony. Without waiting for her to answer, she squeezed into the empty space. As she was trying to get her child out of the stroller, one of the bigger kids she'd come in with bumped into it as he ran by.

"Melvin, Calvin, I'm gonna bust y'all asses for you if you don't stop running around in here like y'all ain't got no home training!" she shouted across the room, drawing distasteful stares. I don't know what y'all looking at? You need to tend to your own damn kids and don't worry about how I talk to mine."

"Are all of them yours?" Ebony hadn't meant to ask, but she couldn't help herself.

The girl gave her an offended look. "Hell no! Calvin is my other baby daddy's son; the rest are mine. Ain't no way in the hell I'm gonna be running around five kids," the girl said as if the idea was that far-fetched.

"Sorry," Ebony said and went back to her paperwork.

The girl nudged her. "You have a pen? They always want you to fill some shit out but ain't never got nothing to write with."

"Here you go." Ebony handed the girl one of the pens from her purse. She looked for her iPod to avoid the conversation the girl was surely about to start up, but realized Tony had taken it.

"You know every time I come to this place it is overcrowded," the girl continued. "It seems like there's always more people than there are workers. You would think that with all the money the city makes they could hire somebody to come in here and help out, you know what I'm saying?"

"Yeah," Ebony said and focused on her paperwork.

"They put us through all this bullshit for that little bit of food stamps and expect us to live off it. They think that we just supposed to smile and take it. I say fuck all that shit. The only reason I even put up with these nasty attitude bitches is because I get almost nine hundred dollars in food stamps every month on the 12th. If it wasn't for that I would've told all these bitches to kiss my ass!"

"Can you keep your voice down please?" a skinny white lady shouted from across the room.

"If you wasn't over there trying to be nosey then your ass wouldn't hear what me and my homegirl were talking about!" the girl shot back. "These bitches be killing me the way they run around up in here like they the Kim Kardashian or some shit, you feel me, girl?" She held up her hand for a high five but Ebony just looked at her. "Oh, I know you ain't in here trying to be cute after I just stuck up for you when that white bitch tried to check your ass?"

"I wasn't trying to be anything. I'm just sitting here filling out my paperwork like everybody else."

"Ex-act-ly." The girl snapped her fingers three times while she enunciated the word. "Your ass is in here trying to get on welfare like everybody else so I don't know why you're trying to front like you're better than us, flinging your dreads and shit like you're cute. You fake as hell."

"Little girl, I've had about enough of your mouth." Ebony stood up and the girl stood up with her.

"What, you got some frog in you? I'll get it popping in this bitch real quick!"

"Miss, are these your kids?" one of the guards had Calvin and Melvin by the arms.

"Yeah, those are my kids and you need to take your hands off of them before I sue you and this whole muthafucker security guard!" she said indignantly and snatched her kids out of the guard's grip hold of her kids. "Y'all bring your bad asses over here. That fat fucker didn't touch you, did he?"

"No, mama," the boys said in unison.

"Good because I'd hate to have to go up top in here. What were you doing to my kids?" She snapped at the guard.

Unlike Ebony, the guard didn't have a whole lot of patience. He kept smiling for anyone who may have been watching, but his tone was sharp and direct when he spoke. "First of all, I wasn't doing anything to these bad ass kids of yours. Second of all, they stuffed paper towels in the urinals in the bathroom and flooded the men's whole bathroom. Now if you don't keep a leash on these monkeys and curb that nasty ass mouth of yours, I'm gonna see that you get thrown out of here today and every time you come back I'll fix it so you're the last person seen for today. Y'all have a nice day!" the guard capped and walked away.

"Fake ass flashlight cop," the girl mumbled as the guard walked away. "And I don't know why I can't never go nowhere without y'all acting a fucking fool and embarrassing me." She gave both boys a good slap across the head. "Now go sit your asses down before I let social service have you the next time they come to my house."

Ebony knew for a fact that she couldn't endure the ignorant young girl or her kids for a moment longer, but thankfully she didn't have to because they were calling her name. By the time Ebony finally got seen and left the building it was 3:40 p.m. She was ready to pull her hair out at the roots. As if the ordeal with the girl hadn't been trying enough, the hoops they made her jump through to recertify her for food stamps were too much. After filling out the stacks of papers and running back and forth to the copy machine at the corner market store to Xerox the documents they needed, she was informed that her case worker had already left for the day and she would have to come back tomorrow. It took all of her resolve to keep from spitting on the woman behind the clerk's desk for not telling her that in the first place. Now she found herself standing in the middle of the street aggravated, broke, and she still had to find a way to come up with dinner for her and Tony.

As she passed Buddy Pawn shop, she looked down at her bracelet on her wrist that her father got for her on her 16th birthday and paused. She cherished the tennis bracelet but at that point eating took precedence over material things. With a lump in her throat she went inside and pawned the bracelet. They only gave her a quarter of what it was worth but at least she and her son would be able to get by until she got things straight with her case worker. She was beyond disgusted with not only the way her day was going but with how her life was playing out. She had considered throwing herself into traffic, but decided against it because her life insurance had lapsed and she couldn't bear the thought of leaving her son worse off than he already was.

She was too depressed to go back home and stare at the walls, so she figured she would walk the streets for a while until she thought of something; this is when Smoke's invitation came to her. Before they had parted company he had invited her to meet him that evening at the bowling alley on 7th Street for some dinner. She had intended to blow it off but after the day she had a good strong drink and that's what she needed. The clock on the side of the bank read 4:00 p.m. so she figured if she hurried she would still be able to meet him at the bowling alley by 5:30 p.m. Adding pep to her steps, she headed toward the city bus.

She arrived at the bowling alley thirty minutes later. The bowling alley wasn't much to look at but the atmosphere was cool and the drinks were potent. The pool table is what started the party off. Smoke introduced Ebony around to his three friends and their ladies. For the most part everybody was cool, except July's wife—Misty—who Ebony kept catching dirty looks from as they were setting up their tables.

"Don't pay her any mind," Smoke whispered in her ear as he brought two pool sticks and two Corona beers to the table. He had beer for him and her. "Misty is always like that around new females."

"Oh, so you bring a lot of bitches around her?" Ebony asked, leaning on her pool cue.

"Only the special ones." Smoke winked and leaned over the table to break, but Ebony laid her pool stick across the pool table on top of his.

"Whatever happened to ladies first?"

"You're correct, where are my manners?" He gave her a mock bow and stepped out of the way. He watched intently as Ebony bent over the pool table, giving him the perfect view of her round little ass. She must've felt his eyes on her because she wiggled it flirtatiously as her pool stick collided with the cue ball.

"Not bad," he said as he watched several of the balls scurry into different holes.

"You could learn a thing or two from me." She sauntered over to the other side of the table and leaned over to take her next shot.

"I could probably teach you a thing or two." He pressed himself against her, taking away her concentration.

So now you gonna cheat to win, huh?" She pushed her round ass into his waist as she tried again to align the stick with the cue ball. Feeling his dick through his jeans made her smile wickedly.

"I'm down to do whatever it takes to win the prize, baby," he said seriously. He looked behind him to see July and Terry watching him. July gave him a wink, which Misty caught and punched him in his ribs. "You gonna cause a small situation in here, baby," Smoke whispered to her.

Ebony looked over her shoulder and saw the girls glaring at her and whispering among themselves. "Some bitches don't have anything better to do than hate," she said and sank her next shot in the pocket.

He flashed July a stern look to check his wife, to which he just shrugged also. "If I were a woman I'd hale your fine ass too," he told her jokingly.

"For what, nigga? I wear jeans and sneakers most of the time and I don't bother with makeup or a hairdresser so there's nothing glamorous about me." She sipped her Corona and looked for her next pool shot.

"That's just it, you shine without trying to," he said. "Ebony, I know women that take many hours getting themselves ready to go out, but you can roll out of bed and still look more beautiful than them."

"What, someone paying you to compliment me?"

"Nah, a dude still talking sweet after he got the pussy." She laughed and leaned over the pool table to drop two balls in the side pocket.

"You stay with jokes." He shoved her playfully and made her miss the next shot.

"You gotta laugh at something or you'll cry over everything," she told him before sinking the next shot. For the next hour or so they sipped and flirted over two games of pool, with her winning the first one and he barely won the second game.

"You're a lot better at pool than you let on, baby," he said, tapping his pool stick on the floor.

"You got lucky the last game," she boasted.

"So then let's shoot the tiebreaker, double or nothing."

She sized him up. "I didn't realize we were gambling."

Smoke invaded her space and whispered directly onto her lips with a kiss, "Everything in life is a gamble."

The scent of liquor mingled with desire on Smoke's breath made the hair on the back of her neck stand up. "I gotta use the restroom," she said, backing up. "Rack 'em, I'll be right back in a minute." She made hurried steps toward the restroom trying to put as much distance between her and Smoke's charismatic ass as possible. Between the liquor and the magnetic attraction between them, her mind was starting to go places it had no business going and voyeurism had never been her thing.

When she got in the cramped ladies room, Misty and the other girls were having an intense discussion. When they noticed Ebony, everyone got quiet. Ebony rolled her eyes and cut through the sea of scornful glares into the stall where she slammed the door and squatted over the bowl to relieve herself. Through the stall door she could hear the humming of their voices like worker bees, so she focused as they kept talking about who she assumed to be her.

"That shit is just so trifling," she could hear Misty saying to someone.

"Fuck that, I'd tell. If that creep ass nigga is doing it and they're all friends there ain't no telling what they're doing in their square time," a third girl chimed in the conversation. "I know if I ever catch my boyfriend Tubb trying to move like Smoke, his ass belongs to me, you hear me?"

Having heard enough, she wiped herself and came out the stall with her head held high in the air. She had a mean switch in her stride on the way to the sink to wash her hands. She took her time washing her hands and watching the girls through the mirror as they watched her. She dispensed a few of the rough brown paper towels and dried her hands calmly before addressing the girls in the bathroom. "Hey, is there something I can help y'all with?"

"No, it seems like you're helped yourself to enough," a dark-skinned girl said.

"Whose name escaped away from the conversation and what is that supposed to mean?" Ebony poked her chest out. She had never been a fighter and the thick dark-skinned girl looked like she would mop the floor with her ass, but her mother always taught her to stick up for herself and she wouldn't let the girl know she was scared.

"Nothing," Red said, trying to avoid what she saw coming her direction. The little yellow girl was as much a brawler as her friends, but she would be damned if they would have her in the streets scrapping in her new *Air Jordans* shoes.

"Oh, because I was feeling like there was some type of problem." She rolled her eyes, letting the drinks pump courage into her system. This was all it took to set Misty off.

"You know what? There is a problem and that problem is a little hot-in-the-pants bitches sticking their pussies where they don't belong."

Ebony backed up and looked at her. "Excuse you? Look, you don't know me or nothing about me so you're way out of line at this moment for trying to judge me."

It was Misty's turn to take a step back. "I'm out of line trying to judge you? You're out of pocket for even being here right now! See, women like you get the shit beat out of them because they ain't got no boundaries and no class. I wish I would catch you trying to rub up on July like you're doing that fool ass nigga Smoke. I'd rock you the fucking sleep right now, bitch!"

"Bitch, what? Your mama's a bitch!" Ebony shot back and took a step toward Misty, but the other two ladies jumped in the middle of them.

"Misty, chill, it ain't ya place to check the situation," Red cut in. "We too grown to be fighting in the bathroom over some dick."

"Tell your miserable ass home girl that," Ebony said.

"Slow up, shorty, because I really don't know you like that. You're already starting off on the wrong foot," Red checked Ebony. "You seemed like you crazy cool, but you're confused about a lot of shit and you need to ease up a little. You in here trying to defend Smoke like he's your man is like trying to fit circles into squares."

Ebony sucked her teeth. "If you've got something to say then you need to spit it out now."

Red raised her hands in surrender. "It ain't my place or my business. All I'm gonna tell you is, you need to make sure you know who your enemies are before you fire those shots."

"Whatever, I'm good on the riddles. Since it seems like me being here is causing problems then maybe I need to get up outta here," Ebony said.

"Yeah, you should probably do that, before reality sets in and you realize how much of a fool Smoke is making of you at this moment," Misty said venomously.

Ebony sized Misty up. "Well, a wise bitch would never argue with a fool because you can't tell one from the other from a distance. Y'all be easy." She flung her hair and stormed out of the bathroom.

Misty stood there shaking her head with her nostrils flaring. "Bitches can be so stupid."

"True indeed, but we were all young and stupid at one point. Now let's get back out there and keep our eyes on our men."

When Ebony exited the bathroom, a small crowd had gathered around the entrance way, undoubtedly having overheard the shouting between the girls. In the center of the pack, wearing a confused expression, was Smoke.

"Everything straight?" Smoke asked, but Ebony ignored him and kept walking. He caught up with her near the door. "What's good with you?"

"I should be asking you the same question, Smoke." She looked him up and down. "I was having a fucked up enough day already without your home girls making me feel like I'm some kind of stank bitch."

"Ebony, what are you talking about?"

"I'm talking about those bitches that were in the bathroom making me feel like I'm some kind of home wrecker or something. Smoke, I did that other woman shit when I was young and I'm not trying to go through it again." She took a step, but he stopped her.

"Ebony, you could never be the other anything. Women like you are one of a kind. I don't know what Misty and them bitches said to you in the bathroom, but if it didn't come outta my mouth it ain't the gospel."

"So you don't have a girlfriend?"

Smoke's eye ticked, but he kept his face even.

"Is that what this is all about?" He smirked as if it was nothing. "Ebony, I wouldn't even insult your intelligence by telling you that I've been keeping it in my pants since the last time we were together. Yeah, I got a little situation that ain't really working out, and Misty and them know shorty which is why they're trying to throw shade on you, but don't feed into that."

"Smoke, you could've just kept it one hundred and told me that you were dealing with someone else and let me decide for myself if I still wanted to see you tonight."

"For what? You said yourself that there was nothing more to this than two old friends hanging out so it never crossed my mind to get that deep into it," he said swiftly. "Ebony, we can go back up in there and I'll make Misty and them tell you what it is." He faked toward the door.

"No, you don't have to do all that. I got all the drama I can stand in twenty-four hours. Just take me home."

"You sure? We could go get some dinner or something?" he suggested.

"Nah, I appreciate it, but I'm good. I just wanna get home to my son."

Chapter 10

Smoke dropped Ebony off in the front of her house and told her he would call her later to check on her in a few, to which she just responded with a grunt sound. She hadn't meant to be so snippy with him, but she was still pissed about what had gone down at the bowling alley with them bitches. She wasn't used to excessive amounts of drama, and it had her drained. All she wanted to do was get upstairs to her apartment and crawl under the covers.

As usual, the knockheads were loitering in the front of the apartment. Cash shuffled back and forth in front of the building directing the fiends to the bench on the far end where Gantsa was sitting, looking around nervously. It was obvious to a duck what he was up to. She started to say something to him about it, but decided against it. She could barely deal with her own child, let alone add her two cents in the business of someone else. She had always liked Gantsa. But she knew at that moment that would be the end of his and Tony's friendship. The last thing she needed was her son getting caught up in their bullshit. Posted up in front of the building were Kush and King who were overseeing the operation while Junebug went on a mission.

"What's up, Ebony?" Kush greeted her with his larcenous smile.

"Hey, Kush," she said in an uninterested tone.

"Damn, you look like somebody kicked your dog in the middle of his ass," King said jokingly.

"It sure feels like it, King," she said with a sigh.

"You wanna talk about it?"

"Not really, I just wanna get upstairs and get in my bed."

"You need some company?" Kush asked.

She looked at him crazy in the face. "I don't think so. King, have you seen Tony? I've been calling him for the last hour or so to see if he made it in from school yet but he didn't answer."

"Yeah, I saw him in the apartments about an hour or so ago."

"Thanks," she said, continuing into the building.

"Ebony, if you change your mind you know where to find me," Kush called after her, but she ignored him to the fullest.

When she got into her apartment, she tripped over Tony's book bag that he had dropped in the middle of the floor, which she had constantly asked him to stop doing. Talking to him was about as effective as talking to a brick wall and it was getting on her last nerves. She snatched the bag off the floor and stormed toward his bedroom. Tony's room was a mess with dirty clothes and dishes on the floor. The boy lay across the bed playing a video game as if he didn't even notice the filth.

"Tony, how many times do I have to tell you about cleaning up behind yourself?" She threw the book bag on the bed.

"My fault," he said nonchalantly.

"And where the hell you been? I've been trying to call you for an hour now."

"I got here a while ago. I saw your missed calls on the caller ID," he told her, never taking his eyes off the video game.

Ebony stepped between him and the television. "Then why didn't you call me back?"

"Because the phone is cut off one way, and so is the internet and the cable!" he said with an attitude.

She cursed silently. She had gotten the notice about the interruption of services from AT&T, but she couldn't pay them and still have carfare to get back and forth to her appointments. She intended to call them and try to get an extension, but with everything going on it slipped her mind.

"Damn, I'm sorry. I'll call them in the morning and take care of it," she said.

"With what?" he asked sarcastically.

"You let me worry about that. Did you do your homework yet?"

"I'll do it later."

"Tony, you know the rules, no video games or television until you've done your homework." She turned the game off.

"Damn, you didn't even give me a chance to save my season!" he barked.

"You'd better watch your fucking mouth, before I bust you in it," she warned. "I don't know what this chip is you've been carrying around on your shoulder the last few weeks, but you'd better get it together before we have a major problem."

"Wouldn't want that. We've got enough problems as it is," he said and opened up his book to do his homework. Ebony started to get in his ass, but someone knocked at the front door and saved him.

She went to the front door and looked through the peephole where she saw two men wearing black coveralls. "Yes?" She opened the front door.

"How are you doing? We're from Small Rent One. We've come for the television and entertainment system you were renting from us." He looked at the clipboard to double check the information. "You're late on your payments."

"Oh, yeah . . . listen, I meant to call you guys about that. I understand I'm a little behind, but if you'll give me another week or two I'll mail you a check," she lied, hoping he would buy it.

He didn't. "Sorry, but you haven't made a payment in five months, so we gotta collect those items."

"C'mon, just give me a little more time and I promise, promise that I'll straighten it out," she pleaded.

The men looked at her sympathetically. "I wish I could, lady, but I could lose my job if I don't collect this stuff. I'm really sorry."

She sighed. "Not as sorry as I am." She opened the door to let them all the way in the house. As the repo men were collecting her entertainment system, Tony bumped past them into the hallway.

"Tony, where are you going?"

"To the corner store, I'll be back," he said without stopping.

"Tony, get your black ass back in here and do your homework," she called after him many times, but he kept going. "Boy, do you hear your mama?" She thought about following him, but the sound of something breaking in the living-room distracted her. After they came and left, the repo men had left with half of Ebony's living-room set. Ebony still had the strength to go out and look for her son. Ebony's living room was a reflection of how her soul felt at that moment. She was so distraught that she threw up in the wastebasket. Feeling defeated and broken, Ebony sat in the empty space left by her entertainment system and cried like a baby.

***

"Look at this muthafucker." Kush motioned to Tony who was coming out of the apartment building with his face twisted up.

"What's up, player? You good?" Gantsa asked, sensing that something was wrong with his friend.

"Yeah, I'm cool," Tony lied. Gantsa knew him well enough to see through it, but he wouldn't pry in front of

Kush. "So what up, where it at?" Tony leaned on the fence next to Cash, who was hitting a loud blunt.

"Shit, just doing what we do." Cash gave Tony dap.

"And what we do is illegal, so you need to keep it trucking before your mother comes out here and calls the police on us for trying to corrupt you." Kush shooed.

"Stall him out, Kush. The little nigga is a'ight," Cash said, exhaling weed smoke through his nose. "What up, little homey? You ready for round two?" He extended the blunt. To everyone's—especially Kush's—surprise Tony hit the blunt like a champ. He damn near choked to death but they appreciated his zeal.

"Little man trying to grow up, huh?" Kush said, looking him up and down.

"Ain't no men in my crib, so I guess the job falls to me," Tony told Kush.

"Where the fuck did you pick that up, on a straight struggle CD?"

Kush narrowed his eyes. "What you got cooking in that big ass brain of yours?"

"A come up," Tony said seriously.

"Tony, I heard that Mr. Troy Davis is paying to tutor little kids. As smart as you are, I know you can land the gig," Gantsa told him.

Tony gave Gantsa a blank stare. "My nigga, do I look like I'm trying to bust my brain for the shorts they're giving out? Nah, I need to get some real money." He looked at Kush punk ass.

Kush waved him off. "Fuck outta here with that lame shit you talking."

"Kush, I'm dead ass serious. I'm stepping to you on some gangsta shit out of respect because this is your block. A bird nigga would've just tried to come out with little work and hustle around you, but I ain't off that."

Kush laughed. "You hear this square ass nigga?" He stepped directly in front of Tony in an attempt to intimidate him. He could tell the boy was scared, but he wouldn't back down. "Son, this ain't summer youth. This is the trap."

"It's also where the money is," Tony told him. "Kush, y'all have known me almost all my life so you know my story. Me and mom's love are barely getting by and I'm tired of sitting on my ass watching her struggle. I need to make a play."

The hunger behind Tony's eyes drew a broad smile to Kush's face. He reached in his pocket and pulled out a few loose bags of rocks, and tested the weight in his hand. "You really trying to get out here and get it up?"

"Come on, Kush, you know Tony don't—" Gantsa began, but Kush silenced him with a look.

"I asked you a question," Kush shook the cracks in his hand. In response Tony held out his hand. "Bet." Kush dropped the bags in his hand. "Let me see how you handle yourself with getting those off, we'll talk." Like a trained soldier Tony spun on his heels and walked toward the building. Kush watched him comically and shook his head.

"Kush, do you think that was a great idea? If he gets knocked, his moms is gonna go through the roof," Gantsa pointed out.

"If he gets knocked he ain't got nobody but himself to blame. He asked for those rocks. I didn't offer them," Kush said.

"Man, you crazy for putting that nigga down. King is gonna wild the fuck out when he finds out." Cash shook his head.

"Man, who the fuck is out there holding this down, me or King?" Kush snapped. "If a little nigga wanna feed his people, who the fuck am I to stop him if I got enough food on my plate for everybody to eat? Cash, I don't know why you and this little bitch nigga Gantsa worrying so much for anyhow. After about thirty minutes of standing in that lobby Tony is either gonna get spooked or tired and run back upstairs."

"You ain't never lied." Cash nodded behind Kush at Tony who was coming back out of the building.

"What's the matter, you heard somebody getting off the elevator and thought it was niggas?" Kush teased him.

"Nah, I'm finished, let me get a few more." Tony held his hand out.

Kush gave him a disbelieving look. "How the hell did you get off fifteen bags in sixty damn seconds when I didn't even see anybody go in the building?"

"Because I know people on the first floor who smoke, they just keep it quiet. They bought six apiece and shorty from the sixth floor is waiting for me to come back with three more because she wanted five. Let's get this money."

***

Ebony lay on Smoke's futon watching TV while sipping a glass of white wine. She had found herself spending quite a bit of time with him over the last few days. As soon as Smoke had heard what happened with Ebony's phone and internet, he had them reconnected. Smoke was turning out to be the only bright spot in her dark days and because of this shit she found herself open all over again.

"Babe, I'm about to run to the corner store right quick, you need anything?" Smoke asked, slipping his Gucci jacket on.

"Yeah, bring me back an orange soda and a bag of onion and garlic chips," Ebony told him and rolled back on her stomach to watch her show on TV.

"And what're you gonna give me for it?" Smoke slapped her across the ass playfully.

"I thought you were done for a while after round two, big daddy," she said playfully, running her foot over his dick through his jeans.

"I can never get enough of that sweetness you got between those thighs." Smoke spread her legs and stuck his face in her pussy.

"You're so nasty." She rolled to the other side of the futon and out of his reach.

"You ain't seen nasty yet. Wait until I get you to Atlanta in a few weeks. I'm gonna really show you nasty, then."

Ebony frowned. "Smoke, why do you play so much?"

Ain't nobody playing, I'm serious. You've been having a rough time of it lately, Ebony, and you deserve for someone to do something nice for you every once in a while. I've got some time off coming and I think ATL would be a great place to spend it. It'll be even more special if I had someone to share it with."

"And what am I supposed to do with my son while we're traveling?" She wanted to know.

"He's a big boy and we'll only be gone for a weekend. Couldn't you get one of your friends to check in on him from time to time while we're gone?"

"Smoke, I'm not gonna just leave my son like that, especially not in the projects we live in. I don't play those types of games."

"A'ight, so maybe we take him with us? You said you've been worried about him being on the block, so why not get him out of the hood for a weekend to open him up to something new. The culture will do him good."

"I don't know, Smoke. You and me doing us is one thing but it may be a little soon to be bringing my son into it," she said. One thing she didn't do was bring men around her kid who she was still unsure about.

"Damn, treat a nigga like a stranger, why, don't ya?" Smoke shook his head.

"I'm sorry, baby. I didn't mean it like that." She crawled up on her knees and hugged him. "Smoke, you've been a godsend to me and I don't know how I would've made it through some of this stuff without your shoulder to cry on, but there's more than just me to think about, and you've got situations to deal with."

"See, I knew you fed into that bullshit Misty and them were kicking at the pool hall," Smoke said hostilely.

"First of all, I didn't feed into shit, I'm just calling it like I see it. Smoke, you said yourself that you've another situation that hasn't been completely resolved so it doesn't make any sense to get too deep into another situation before you've cleaned up the first one."

Smoke clutched his head like she was giving him a headache. "Ebony, I want you to trust me but you gotta be willing to let me in. Don't answer me about Atlanta now, give it some thought, then get back, okay?" Ebony nodded. "Good. Now I'm going to the store." Smoke left the apartment.

Ebony lay there for a minute and contemplated Smoke's offer. For as bad as she would've loved an all-expenses paid trip to ATL, she knew the timing was wrong. Tony seemed to be becoming more belligerent by the day, questioning her when she told him something and hanging in front of the apartments every time her back was turned. The neighbors were even whispering that Tony might be selling drugs for Junebug, but she didn't believe her son had slipped that far yet. Tony was feeling himself and she needed to find a way to slow him down. Thinking of Tony made her realize that she hadn't spoken to him in a few hours. Smoke had left his cell phone on the table, so she decided to use it to call Tony. As she was flipping the phone open, another call was coming through, so she ended up answering the phone by accident.

"Hello? Hello? Hello?" She could hear a feminine voice coming over the phone line. She looked at the caller ID screen and it read '*home.*' "I hope this ain't one of Smoke's bitches playing on the phone. I keep telling you little bitches about staying in your lane, but I can see that I'm gonna have to show you . . . again. Is anybody there?" Not really sure what to do, Ebony hung up the phone.

For a long period of time she just sat there holding the phone. She had completely forgotten that she was supposed to be calling Tony as her mind tried to make heads or tails out of the situation she had allowed herself to walk into. She shouldn't have been surprised by something like this going with Smoke, especially after the thing Misty and the other girl were saying to her. The phone rang three more times, twice were from *home* again and once from a block number. She just ignored it and slipped her clothes on.

Smoke finally came back from the store looking like he had run both ways. Dropping the bags on the floor, he began to search the room. "Looking for this?" She held the phone up and as she did it started ringing again. She looked at the word *home* on the caller ID and handed the phone to Smoke. "It's for you."

"Ebony, I can explain . . ." he began, but she didn't want to hear it.

"No need, Smoke. I know just how this movie going play out," she said emotionally.

"Babe, it ain't like you think."

She looked at him as if he had lost his fucking mind. "What the fuck do you mean it ain't like that? Smoke, you had the number stored as *home* in your phone. I might not have gotten my degree, but I'm not an idiot. Smoke, just say that you live with a bitch!"

"Okay, I live with a broad, but it's complicated, Ebony." Smoke tried to plead his case, but Ebony didn't need to hear it.

"Trust me, baby, I know all about it. You and Shorty are on the outs and it's looking like y'all are headed for a breakup, right?"

"Ebony . . ." he began.

"Smoke, please stop. Anything else that comes out of your mouth is gonna be a lie so save your tongue and my ears the speech," she said, calmly pulled her dreads into a ponytail. "I told you from the gate that all you had to do was keep it one hundred with me, but you couldn't do that, could you? Men amaze me because they'd rather lie and risk a problem than telling the truth and letting the chips fall where they will."

"So you would've still fucked with me if I had told you that I was living with another woman who I'm not fucking?" he asked.

"No, because that shit sounds crazy. Smoke, we had fun, but I guess at the end of the day it is what it is."

"So you're just gonna walk out on what we have without even giving me the benefit of the doubt?" Smoke called after her.

"Smoke, what do we have except a bunch of problems and lies? I've got enough problems of my own without you adding to it, man." Ebony felt herself get emotional so she cut it short. "It's been fun, Smoke, but I deserve better than what you're offering."

"Hold on, Ebony. It's late so at least let me give you a ride back to your block." He grabbed her by the arm trying to stop her.

Ebony jerked away and gave him a look that made him take a few steps back.

"Smoke, please don't pick now to start acting like you care about me. I'll be fine on the city bus." She closed the door softly behind her.

Chapter 11

Junebug threw the fourth grenade that was taped to a gas station can. Then ran to meet Candice at the mansion's long driveway. They reached the Benz at the same time.

"You really think he's going to go for it? He can't be that dumb!" Junebug said as he caught his breath. Candice looked into his brown eyes as she responded.

"Play the odds, baby. We took North, West, and South leaving the only exit being East, the garage. Plus, he strikes me as the cowardly type," she said, leaning towards Junebug, looking into his eyes.

"Leaving it to you, unh?" he asked sarcastically. She was inches from his face when they finally kissed. Their lips locked as hungry tongues met in the middle. Candice released her MP-5, and grabbed his dick through his jeans. Things were getting hot and heavy when the fourth explosion sent debris raining down over them. Candice tensed, anticipating it, and giggled as it stopped.

"Pardon my language, but you're a sick bitch!" said Junebug as he stood there. He then gave her his hand and helped her up. She twisted her face up in protest at the word *bitch*. "But you're cute and sexy as hell."

"Shut up and go finish this nigga off," she replied, shaking the dirt and rocks from her hair. Junebug pulled the RPG from the big bag and headed to finish off Moe.

Moe hit the garage door, opening from his cell phone, exposing them to the chilly and smoke-filled night air.

"What are you waiting on? Let's go!" urged Moe. '40,' barely turned the key when lighting and thunder caused his heart to jump. Moe thought he was in a 70's movie, or a bad dream. His ears rang as he coughed, and the truck's cabin filled with smoke. 40 was awake, but he was dazed and pinned against the seat by the steering wheel. Moe himself was disorientated by the blast. The rear of the truck was at the Maserati next to them. He knew his men were of no help and he had to get out quickly. He attempted to open the door and then tried to kick it open. On the third try he succeeded. The fresh air thick with smoke, he saw that his custom Wrangler jeep was undamaged. Walking towards it, his eyes started to focus just as the ringing in his ears died down. On the way to the Wrangler he even thought of going for his motorcycle. That's when he noticed movement to his left. It was two figures walking side by side—a man and a woman. The woman was lifting something to her shoulder level. The assassin bitch! Bullets hit the Yukon and the Wrangler as he dove for cover. He only had matching black baby Desert Eagles, but he was steady.

"This can't be it. Is there a hanger, or building on the property?" asked Candice, shoving a clip into an old police-issued Glock 17.

"Yeah, on the far end. I think we can make it!" replied Loud, calling his drivers so that they were on the same page. Until Junebug interrupted him.

"Wait, one of them is coming," said Junebug.

"Yeah, he looks unarmed." Although he was dressed for war in all-black, with gloves, a flak vest, and boots, his assault rifle was slung over his shoulder, both hands up.

"Wonder what's his game," whispered Candice.

"Mi jefe hablar," the Mexican yelled loudly. Spanish confused everyone except Junebug and Candice."

"What this muthafucka saying?" shouted Loud as he gripped his 9mm Desert Eagle gun.

"Did he just call us whores?"

"No, he said his boss wants to talk," said Junebug, slipping out of the truck. "Cover me. If they start letting off shots, don't worry about me. Just get Candice back to the plane and to Arkansas."

"Junebug, wait!" screamed Candice, reaching for her door.

"No! If they wanted to kill us they wouldn't have sent a man to talk," Junebug said, stepping into the Louisiana humidity.

Chapter 12

"Just make it back to me," wept Candice, a single tear pouring on her eyelid. Junebug was searched twice by two different men before he made it inside of the air-conditioned Sprinter van. By the weight of the doors, he knew the RV sized van was armored, and well protected by the soldiers in the motorcade. Inside sat one Hispanic man immaculately dressed in expensive denim jeans and an equally expensive long-sleeved button-up with blue alligator skin cowboy boots. Across from Junebug was a 42-inch flat screen with a feed from outside cameras broken up into four sections. They were so advanced one was zoomed into Loud's Range Rover and was looking at Candice's face. The Hispanic man noticed him looking and decided to speak.

"Do you know who I am?" he asked, sipping his drink.

"Don't flatter yourself, I have no idea!" replied Junebug. The man smiled, laughing tightly.

"You sure?" Blast pointed his finger at him then stroked his goatee.

"I've seen you once before at Peanut's yacht, right?" Junebug asked.

The man nodded yes.

"What do you want? You work for him?" asked Blast.

He shook his head. "Yes, that's my brother, said Junebug.

"You waste no time, do you? The name's Blast, and I want you to work with me. I've known about you and your brother for some time now. You handle business as if you came up in the cartel. I have a proposal for you." Blast sipped his drink slowly. "If you game?"

"I'm done working for anyone, especially the Cartel, I—" declared Junebug.

Upset that he left Candice, Junebug went inside to talk to Blast. Moe was tied up and being watched over by Candice. Suddenly, Junebug was struck by several hard blows to the chest and stomach. *This is it*, he thought. He then checked his waist band for a handgun and came up blank, realizing he had left it and his AK in the truck. Blast took off running while Moe peeked around the corner, leaving the area where Candice remained.

"Junebug, wait!" Candice screamed.

Candice ripped shots at Moe but missed.

Someone shouted from inside the garage.

"Junebug, wait, you hear that?" asked Candice. He looked at her and smirked sarcastically, before walking out the front door to avoid being shot or getting Candice killed.

Candice was right behind him now, firing shots back into the garage as she exited.

Breathing heavily, Junebug remarked, "Girl, you're crazy!"

***

Candice stared at Junebug as he pulled into a small hotel in Columbia, Missouri. Junebug was prepared to drive all the way to the Gulf of Mexico just to catch up to Loud. But Candice insisted they sleep on it, and come up with a better plan. Junebug needed the guns, but decided to take a risk and called in a favor to a cuz of Sarah's in Louisiana by the name of Tammy. While Junebug finalized things and arranged a flight with the crew of his privately owned G5 Learjet, Candice finished up in the shower. She took a seat on the bed still wrapped in a large brown towel. She eyed Junebug as she lotioned up, opening her legs as she moisturized her thighs, revealing her freshly shaved pussy. Once she finished up, she went to him. "So, Junebug baby, what are you going to do once this done?"

He was preoccupied with murder, keeping himself alive, fucking her, and mourning his brother and first love. Confused, he remained silent.

"Come on, talk, Junebug?" urged Candice.

"First, I've got to bury my family members. They're getting a proper funeral." He paused.

"With due respect, then what?"

"I guess we'll find a place to live maybe in the south." She pushed him down on the bed and pinned him with a kiss.

"Let's go to South America, or Africa. It'll be great." Junebug thought it over as he noticed how perfect her chocolate skin was.

"You been watchin' *Belly*, or some shit? My name is Consequence, not Sincere." He laughed. But for real I've had enough Hispanics for a lifetime. Asia or Africa?"

Candice perked up and kissed him.

"For real, babe?" Her eyes opened in a display of appreciation. "Please, Junebug."

"Yes, for real. I've got enough money to build us a house on each continent. So whatever you want." Silently, Candice stared into his eyes, unbelieving.

"What?" asked Junebug. "I don't—" he got out before she quieted him, placing her fingers over his lips.

"Don't lie, don't make excuses, and I'll rephrase it, because I know your love for your last girlfriend is still fresh. Will I ever have your heart?" she asked patiently.

It didn't take much thought on his behalf. "Yes, one day it will be." She smiled hearing that.

"Schedule the flight plans then, daddy," Candice teased in the voice of a hood chick. She sounded almost too hood, Junebug thought as his dick disappeared into her deep throat. But he took his mind off of it.

She sipped chilled Ace of Spades, and shared a few strawberries with him as they sailed over Arkansas on the way to the private air strip in Louisiana. He had placed 21 million dollars in cash on the plane, so they could go to Brazil, and from there Africa.

"You think we'll be good, Junebug?"

"Yeah, as long as we work together and use the element of surprise. We'll be Gucci!" He replied with a smirk.

"I mean, good together, silly."

Junebug scooted closer to her, inhaling her essences before he spoke. "I know things are moving fast, but yes. We will be. Not to dismiss your concerns, but this convo can wait. Let's focus on Consequence, because the one thing I know is he won't be as easy as Moe."

Candice laughed with confidence bordering on arrogance.

"Baby, you got me. You're seen only a tiny bit of what I can do."

Junebug shook his head. "Candice, you don't know Consequence. He's got about twenty of you, plus a small army at his beck and call. We're gonna need a lot of luck, and even more bullets to pull this off."

This revelation quieted Candice, allowing her to process her thoughts of how she should proceed. Just as the pilot announced 20 minutes till landfall, Junebug only wondered about what kind of arsenal they had. He hoped it wasn't junk.

When the jet landed, Loud was waiting with a small three-vehicle convoy. Tossing their small duffle bags into Loud's Range Rover, Junebug opened the rear available arsenal. Obliging, Loud opened the rear hatch on the Range Rover, revealing a large duffle bag, two hard cases, and a single coat. Inside were two semi-automatic AR-15s, an assortment of handguns with extended magazines and ammo. The most impressive piece was the Saiga-12 semi-automatic shotgun, but it only had the standard 2 shot ag, not the 30 shot, or 50 shot drum.

Sadly disappointed, Candice shook her head. Junebug voiced his dissatisfaction.

"Fuck I'm doing with this, Loud?" he asked, tossing a slightly rusted 1911 Smith and Wesson back into the duffle bag. "I wouldn't have used any of this shit in my teenage years," said Junebug as Candice inspected the weapons. Loud shrugged.

"You just called last night. I can do better, but I need time."

"We'll wait, we need military grade weapons," said Candice. Junebug looked at her. "How much time, Loud?"

"At least 2-4 days, but it'll cost you."

"Do what you can today. I'll pay double. I don't have two days. Now let's go see those men you got for me." Loud closed the hatch then got in the front passenger seat of the Range Rover while Junebug and Candice were seated in the rear. Driving off the tarmac, they drove towards the front gates, as Junebug emailed the jet's crew with instructions. Within seconds Candice broke his concentration.

"Junebug! Look! Junebug!" she shouted excitedly.

He looked up in time to see at least 4 to 5 large black SUVs and a single silver Benz Sprinter van. Loud's man slammed on his brakes, just yards away. Immediately, armed Hispanic men poured from the vehicle, took up their positions, and aimed at their small convoy. Candice dove over the seat for a weapon and found them all empty. Things were already starting off poorly.

Blast laughed to himself as he lit his Cuban cigar while he conveniently watched Junebug's small convoy come to a complete stop at the roadblock his men initiated. He sipped Patron Platinum from the safety of the level's armored Sprinter, and watched the situation play out. All the information Gantsa had given him was on point. Allowing him to blackmail and pay off Junebug's pilot, getting Junebug's flight plans. He had ample opportunity to kill Junebug, but that wasn't beneficial to Blast, off his pockets.

He ran his empire like a true heartless mogul. So why kill him then try to replace him, was Blast's reasoning. As long as Junebug wasn't loyal to Blast after he tried to assassinate him, he could live. After all, you don't fire the CEOs of successful businesses that turn consistent profits during a corporate takeover, or buy out.

"Tell them that I just want to talk. There's no need for bloodshed!" said Blast through a walkie-talkie.

Pissed, Candice and Junebug got a couple of the better guns loaded as they considered their options.

"Is there another way out, Loud?" asked Consequence as he placed a Colt .45 on his hip that had seen better days. Loud shook his head.

"Not unless we drive through the river towards the rear of the strip. We're surrounded by Federal Marshals and I lost my girlfriend to this shit. Find someone else." All that got Junebug was another sip and a grin on his face.

"What if I cut the price and give you the man that betrayed you, unh? Would you do it then?" asked Blast.

"Not for a billion dollars, and Mustafa's head."

"You know Mustafa sent me to kill you. I could take over North America. The only reason I'm giving you this opportunity is because I'd hate to replace you, or change what's already perfect. In short, if you out I could kill you and move on. There's at least a half a million more mayates that would kill to replace you. You sure you want to tell me no?"

Junebug felt the weight of the threat, but he knew if you stood for nothing you fall for anything. His idea of a man was: you make and create your own destiny.

"Yep. I'm good."

Blast simply nodded and looked at the screen that held Candice's image, and 100 men came in closer.

"You know if you refuse me, and I decided to kill you, my men will kill your crew. Which is for the best for her sake? I'm sure she'll run out of ammo, and they'll take her alive."

Blast let Junebug draw his own conclusion before he said, "She may just like it. I hear Mendoza's got a dick like an elephant trunk. Unless you've got a better play, that's it for you." In silence Junebug considered every possible outcome as if it was a game of chess. Every move ended in a checkmate. His last and best option was try to negotiate with Blast and hope he could come to terms with him.

"Listen, Blast, I get what you want, and that's to kill Mustafa. I can't and won't stay in the game after this. I still have a few men in place in Arkansas. I'll personally see to it that they are brought up to speed. That's it and that's all." Blast spun his glass in between his fingers over the oak and marble veneer table and pondered the offer, then looked at the screen, eyeing Candice openly before he spoke.

"Deal, but I got you for one month," Blast said.

"One last thing. We need guns if you want us to help with Mustafa."

"Not a problem."

"She's not your fucking business for the record."

Blast smiled.

"Blast, your chick is more than she lets on. I ran a check on her through my CIA connections. The training she's received over the last years is far beyond that of a common cop. The most suspicious thing is she doesn't have a birth certificate, or even a social security number." Junebug stared into the screen and thought about what he really knew about Candice. It amounted to nothing. The love she shared with him was very real. Their sex was very real and passionate. Plus, Blast was just as much a mystery as she was.

"She's my problem."

"Yes, she is, my friend."

"I'm not your friend. Now let's go handle this nigga Mustafa."

***

With the weekend bus schedule it took Ebony over 2 ½ hours to get home. She didn't mind the ride though because she needed the time to clear her head. The way things played out with Smoke stung because she was really feeling him, but it could've gone a lot worse. At the end of the day she knew to take it for what it was, a good time. Ebony might not have had a fancy job like she envisioned, or any degrees, but she had a good heart and because of this she knew good things would come to her. When the time was right a man would come along that only saw her and no one else, and until then she would just learn to be happy with herself.

When she crossed South Lily Street, the first thing she noticed was the eerie silence. It was a relatively nice night and no one was on any of the corners. When she crossed the street on Lake, she spotted Kush and Gantsa skulking through the parking lot, with Kush whispering in his ear about the devil knew what. Tucked under Kush's arm was a rolled up brown paper bag.

No matter how far down the rabbit hole Gantsa slipped, Ebony still saw him as the little boy who used to come by the house to play with her son. Blast saw him differently in the hood and it was time to call Gantsa's number up. Seeing what Gantsa was becoming made Ebony thankful for Tony. He could be hard-headed and had mannish ways but at least he wasn't out committing crimes like the rest of the kids in the neighborhood.

Ebony knew she raised her son better than that and felt bad about turning a blind eye to little Gantsa. She was going to make it her business to go and have a talk with Gantsa's aunt about the things he was getting into.

When Ebony made around the corner toward her apartment, she found the courtyard just as empty as the streets. As she walked along, she noticed that several of the streetlights had been busted out as well at the ones in front of her apartment. She almost didn't see King until she was right on top of him.

"Damn, you scared me." Ebony jumped when King peeled from the shadows.

"I'm sorry, Ebony, but I've been trying to find you all day," King said. There was something in his tone that made her uneasy.

"Some shit went down out here earlier between Kush and some niggas from the other side of the hood. There was a major shooting and Tony got caught up on it," King said with a heavy heart.

"Oh, my god, please don't tell me my baby is dead?" She grabbed King by his shirt in tears.

"Ebony, calm down. Tony wasn't shot, he was the shooter!" King informed her.

"What? We don't own a handgun. Where did he get a gun from?" She went on and on to the point where she was almost hysterical. She couldn't imagine her son in jail for murder and even toying with the thought made her nauseous.

"Ebony, I don't have a lot because I wasn't out here. From what I'm hearing some words were exchanged about Junebug and Peanut that escalated to a fistfight. Sometime during the fight Tony came out with a hammer and started banging," King explained.

Ebony shook her head in disbelief. "No, maybe somebody else's kid, but not my son. My child is no killer. He would never even touch a handgun."

"Yeah, well that's what the police said who came and picked him up. Ebony, there was at least a dozen people that saw what went down out here and they all tell the same story."

"Dear my God, I need to sit down." She stumbled over to the benches and took a seat. "How could I have allowed him to get caught up in this foolishness?"

King tried to console her. "Ebony, you didn't get him into anything. Sometimes the call of the streets gets too strong and we answer it."

"This is that muthafucker Kush's fault. I know he roped my son into this shit and I'm gonna kill him." She hopped up off the bench, but King stopped her.

"Ebony, you can't blame somebody else for what Tony decided to do. I made it clear to everyone in the hood that he wasn't to be recruited but if somebody does something voluntarily it falls on them. Tony tried to make his move and took his first knock upside the head. The Dope Boys swooped down on him about four hours ago, so he may still be in there somewhere."

"I've gotta go see about my son." She started off in the direction of the precinct.

"Hold on Ebony, I'll come with you," King offered.

"Thank you, but you and your crew have done enough for me and my son. I'd appreciate it if you stayed away from us. If I catch you or any of your boys talking to my son again I'm calling the white folks," she said coldly.

"Ebony, you know I'd never do anything to hurt Tony." King's voice was thick with emotion.

"Which is just why you're going to let him be," she said and disappeared down the hill.

Chapter 13

Ebony arrived at the Blytheville Police Department. She was notified that due to overcrowding, Tony had been moved. She ended up visiting three precincts in the Ville before finally tracking him down. After filling out the necessary paperwork, the woman behind the desk wearing the sergeant's stripes allowed her a ten-minute visit with Tony. He looked so pitiful sitting in the dirty cell that she broke down and cried like a new born baby. She was upset to see her son behind bars in a dirty cell. "Baby, are you okay?" She held his small hands through the bars.

"Yeah, mother, I'm good," he said, trying to play tough but she could tell he was scared as hell. He was also sporting some fresh cuts and bruises, meaning that he had been roughed up at some point doing the crime.

"What happened? They said you were shooting at some niggas, but I know there has to be some kind of mistake," she said.

"No, it wasn't a mistake, Ma. Some guys had come over to our side of the hood beefing and a big fight broke out. I was scared so I got the handgun out of the grass and started shooting, but you gotta believe me, I wasn't trying to hurt anybody." Tony's eyes began to water.

"Don't you worry. I'm gonna get you outta here as quick as I can tonight," she assured him.

"Ebony, I wouldn't bet on that," a cop who had been ear-hustling interjected. "We've got him at the scene of the crime with the handgun laying at his feet. Furthermore, your son is a part of that drug ring they've got going on in the hood."

"That's impossible . . . my kid doesn't sell drugs," she said indignantly.

The officer looked at her like she was crazy. "Hey, Mike, come here for a minute, will you?" He stopped a plain-clothed officer that was walking by.

"What's up?" the plain-clothed officer asked.

"This lady here says her son doesn't sell drugs."

The plain-clothed officer looked inside the cell and laughed out loud. "Are you kidding me? I've been watching this little dude sell dope for Kush for the last three weekends. He's so good at it we nicknamed him Money Man." The two officers laughed and left her standing there dumbfounded.

"Tony, is what they're saying true?" she asked, but he remained silent. "Boy, you better tell me something before I reach in that cell and choke the shit outta you."

He sucked his teeth. "Yeah, it's true, mom."

She wanted to faint. "Tony, for as many talks as we've had about the streets, what would make you jump out the window and do something so damn stupid?"

"You!" He snapped at her. "Ma, day in and day out I watched you scrape money and borrow food to get us through the next day and that shit was killing me. Every guy you get with disappeared and you are suffering and you gotta pick the pieces up and start all over again, all by yourself. I just wanted to prove to you that I was a man that could do more for you than them sucks you keep falling for."

His words hit her like bricks. With all that had been going on, she had only thought about herself and how hard things were on her. She never once stopped to think of what it was doing to Tony and hearing it from the horse's mouth cut her deeply inside.

"Time is up, Ms.," a uniformed officer notified Ebony that it was time to leave.

"I'm gonna get you out of this place, son," she told him as she was escorted away. She was blinded by tears as she rushed through the precinct lobby toward the exit. Some of the officers who had overheard what was going on looked at her and shook their heads, but the desk sergeant felt sorry for her.

"I'm going on a break," the sergeant said and came from behind the desk. When she got outside, Ebony was sitting on the stairs sobbing. "Here you go." The sergeant handed her a roll of tissue.

"Thank you," she said, dabbing her eyes. "I don't know how this happened. I've done everything I could to be a good mother and it just seems like I'm not doing enough."

"No matter how much we do it never does," the officer told her. "We work our fingers to the bone to make sure our kids have the things we need and they still can't get over not having their need or want in life. Some can fly straight on their own and others need a little coaxing."

"Do you have children too?"

"Yes, three girls, one boy and a husband who is in his second childhood." The officer laughed. "There are times when I wanna beat myself up for the things everybody else does, but I have to remind myself that it's not me doing dumb shit, it's them. You can't get nobody right until you get yourself right, and the first step is learning to love and appreciate you even when no one else does.

"Those are some wise words," Ebony said.

"I've been around long enough to learn from trial and error, Ebony."

Her head snapped up in surprise. "How did you know my name?"

"I know your name from when you showed me your ID, but I know your voice from my husband's voicemail. I'm Teresa, Smoke's wife."

"Oh my God." She covered her mouth in embarrassment. "Teresa, let me explain. I never knew that Smoke was married. We . . ."

"No need to explain, Ebony, because I am so past getting upset with him and his wandering dick. While he's out doing him you can best believe that I'm out doing me. When you came in here and made the connection I started to lose your son's paperwork, but as I listened to what y'all were going through I felt bad."

"Even though I had sex with your husband?"

Teresa nodded. "Ebony, it'd be easy for me to be here trying to put the beats on you for what you've done, but at the end of the day I didn't take those vows with you, I took them with Smoke. You're just a casualty of the sick little games he's been playing for many years. If you're smart, you'll leave him alone for good, but if you're dumb you'll keep getting roped into his apologies like I've been doing for the last few years."

"If you know what kind of nigga he is then why are you still with him?"

"Out of convenience, of course. Smoke is a low-down bitch, but he's got a healthy bank account and owns a few properties. One day I'll wake up and leave him but for now I'm content to let him wonder while I slowly bleed his bank account dry. When he's broke and on his last legs, then I'll kick his ass to the curb with the rest of the trash." This got Ebony to laugh. "Listen, clean yourself up and go get something to eat. By the time you come back I'll have pulled some strings to have your son released to you with a date for y'all to go to family court. I probably can't do anything about the charges he's facing at this moment. At least he can fight his case from the streets and not in jail. Just stay strong because y'all gonna need each other for support."

"Why are you doing this for me?" The woman was walking up the stairs.

She stopped for a minute. "Because I feel sorry for you, Ebony. You think you're a woman and you're just another baby with a baby trying to make it in this world. Come back in a little bit to pick your son up. Don't let me see either one of you again in my jail, because you've used up your last free pass to freedom."

The woman started on Tony's release papers to go home. Twenty-five minutes later, he was processed and ready to go by the time his mother arrived back. She was so excited to see him and tears rolled down her face. She looked around the jail for Teresa to tell her thanks. The person at the desk told Ebony she was gone for the day. She had a family emergency matter to handle. Ebony and her son had a long talk about life and his upcoming court case. They had a hard road ahead of them. They had to be on the same page to face the consequences about to go down. Tony seemed like his stay in a cell had possibly scared some sense into him but only time would tell.

When they got to their apartment building there was a crowd of people gathered in front of it. The police had the whole area taped off and wouldn't let anybody inside. On the ground there was a body covered in a bloody white sheet. Ebony couldn't see the face, but the corpse was wearing a familiar looking sneaker. Near the front of the crowd she spotted Keisha's uncle Big Face and his partner—Chris—whispering among each other.

"What happened?" Ebony asked Big Face.

"The chickens have finally come home to the roost." Big Face nodded at the lobby. The police were bringing Kush and Cash out in handcuffs. Kush was still smirking like it was a game while Cash looked ready to cry. "Them boys they were shooting at earlier came back around with some guns of their own and their aim was just a little bit better."

"Where Gantsa?" Tony asked frantically.

Big Face removed his do-rag and placed it over his heart. "I tried to tell him to find another game" — he looked down sadly at the bloody sheet — "but the young ones never listen."

"No!" Tony collapsed into his mother's arms and screamed over and over into her chest.

She tried to console him as best she could, but there was nothing she could do to soothe his grief. She was both saddened and relieved by the sight of Gantsa laying under that sheet. She was sad because he was a young man with so much potential who just happened to get caught up in Kush's little game, but relieved because she knew that if the wind had blown the other way it would've been her kid under that bloody sheet.

After the trouble with her son, Tony, she decided that she had enough drama. Taking just a few personal items, she packed her and Tony up and went to have a long overdue talk with her parents. She had expected to have to whine and beg, but surprisingly her parents had missed her as much as she had missed them, especially her mother. It was high time that she got to know her grandson and the woman her little girl had grown into. The bus ride took over three hours to get to her parents' house. The little items she had didn't take much room on the bus at all. After all she'd been through selling drugs, dealing with different niggas, she still hadn't learned her lesson. She was at the stage now of not dating a man again and trying something new. The tears falling down her cheeks hurt her mother's heart. Ebony used to the fast life and living off government checks month to month was not going to do it.

Chapter 14

Two years later, Caressa watched closely as Ebony stirred in her sleep. A long yawn escaped her lips. The bright light shining on her face made her lids flutter repeatedly. After struggling blinking for a minute or so, she was finally able to open her eyes completely.

"Good morning, sleepy beauty. Happy birthday."

"Good morning, handsome, and thank you." A slight smile spread across her soft lips. "How long have you been sitting here looking at me?"

"Not long, I just got back from getting us some breakfast, so get up, wash your face, and hit that mouth." They both shared a laugh.

"My breath doesn't stink bitch."

Caressa leaned down and gave her a pop kiss. "Don't matter, I'll still kiss your sexy ass." Grabbing her hand, she helped her from the bed.

After a much needed nap, Ebony woke up to Caressa sliding a long dildo inside her tight pussy from the back. Planting soft kisses on the back of her neck, she slowly stroked her while holding her leg up in the air. As the owner, she watched in delight as Ebony's pussy stuck out like a sore thumb. Ebony was spitting out that tasty cream for Caressa to eat after she was done. Switching positions, Caressa buried her head between Ebony's legs to taste her deliciousness. Aggressively, she attacked Ebony's pussy to stake her claim. She needed Ebony to know that she belonged to her after everything she did *for* her and *to* her. Ebony's body shook as she held the top of Caressa's head.

"What are you doing to me?" Ebony asked, like she didn't know.

"Writing my name inside this pussy is an amazing sight to see." Caressa could feel Ebony's thick legs lock down on her head, but she kept sucking on her big pearl tongue.

"You trying to kill a bitch in here."

"Cum for a real Boss Bitch!"

"I can't, you sucked too good right now."

"I'm not stopping until you bust all on my lips and face down here."

Forcefully, Caressa used both hands to pin Ebony's legs down, going back to attack mode full force. Ebony moaned, bucked, and tried to wiggle away from Caressa, but that wasn't happening. Caressa spent too much time on lockdown in federal prison dreaming about the day she would be able to suck the life out of some pussy. And over the past few months, she decided that Ebony would be the one she gave her tongue, dildo, and soft heart to. She was solid and kept a nigga in a positive space during the end of her journey.

Ebony's body finally gave in and dripped all the good cum on Caressa's tongue. Satisfied, she released her strong grip and sat on her face. She rode her face about ten minutes before changing position. Lying on her back, she slapped Ebony on the thighs. "Get on top and ride it like Megan Thee Stallion. I want your toes curled up, and ass face down." Caressa's dildo was face straight up, so Ebony got on her knees and faced the opposite direction. Her ass was damn near in Caressa's face, but Caressa enjoyed the nice view. Ebony stroked the dildo a few times before Caressa felt her mouth wrap around the clit. Leaning over, she fucked Ebony with her long middle finger until she dripped cum while she spit and choke on Caressa. Once Ebony was standing tall, she saddled up and eased down on it until it disappeared into her tight walls.

Ebony had her knees buckling when she came up to the top and slid back down. The feeling of the dildo caressing the inside of her gushy pussy was euphoric.

"Speed it up," she demanded, while gripping her ass cheeks, so her cum can rush down Caressa's dildo. Playing in her pussy juices, she greased her asshole for some anal surprise. She stuck her thumb inside, making Ebony buck harder like a wild horse. "Ah! Ah! Ah! Baby girl." She fingered her faster. "Bounce on baby girl's big truck toy." Ebony followed every instruction she gave to her.

Ebony turned around and shook her booty in the air before backing up to Caressa while she waited like a hungry hyena. Giving Ebony's asshole a wet kiss and lick, Caressa rubbed her dildo up and down her slit and ass while enjoying the sight of all that darkness. Finally, sticking it in her slippery wet pussy, Caressa fingered her big booty while she arched up higher in the air.

"Spread that ass some more shit." She began to slow stroke, listening to it speak back while she hit that G-spot. Ebony let out a few loud screams while gripping the bed sheets, so Caressa pulled out and planted kisses on her beautiful lower back.

"Ebony, I love you, and tell momma how good I made that pussy feel!"

"So good, baby girl. Put it back inside me," Ebony moaned, displaying a freaky fuck face. "Caressa, I love you too, momma." Ebony whined, looking back over her shoulders at that long dildo pumping deep in them guts.

With both hands on her shoulders, Caressa went harder in the paint like a center for the Lakers. "You gon' have my love forever or what?"

"Yes."

"You sure, bitch?"

"Yes."

"Ohh. Yes." Ebony threw her ass back, and Caressa's thrust matched hers. After drilling her hard and pulling her long hair, Caressa went deep into Ebony's treasure box. Ebony came all over the bed sheets.

As she laid peacefully in Caressa's arms, she couldn't help but to stare in her pretty eyes. Caressa loved everything about Ebony and couldn't risk not seeing her again. Before she left they were going to make arrangements to get her relocated to live with her. She'd been through hell and back dealing with past relationships, going to jail and losing everything she owed from selling drugs in the past. Caressa closed her eyes and drifted off into space in a deep sleep, feeling like a true champion.

***

This discomfort from his recent gun-inflicted wound to the shoulder had Ace tossing and turning. It had been the normal for the past few nights after his visit to the local neighborhood doctor, who normally treated patients who couldn't afford to go to a regular hospital or simply just couldn't go, unless they wanted to go to jail afterwards. The painkiller prescribed by the unlicensed practicing physician he had gone to had done nothing to ease the pain. Instead, the pills had caused Ace to become sick on the stomach. He discontinued taking them, fearing the worst. He chose to fight the excruciating pain off naturally and was not realizing how difficult of a task his decision was. He didn't know how much longer he could take being cooped up in one of his stash cribs, before he actually had to go see a real doctor at a hospital. He was sure the police were looking for him for what happened at the apartments for questioning about the murder of his friend Gantsa.

It had been a while since he had last seen the incident flash across the television screen but he knew it hadn't gone away that easily. Ever since they had captured several other crew members, he had been on edge. He wondered if Moe would dime him out with the police, as being the one who had gotten away in this case. After not hearing any mention of his name on the local news, he was somewhat convinced that despite all that had transpired, he was playing by street rules, and didn't give up. Still, he laid low, cautiously, until he could be certain that was the case. Ace flicked through channel after channel with nothing in particular in mind to watch. He stopped when he reached the BET Network station. He was just about to get into the latest Gucci Mane video when his mind did a quick back track. Subconsciously he thought he had recognized something or rather someone a few channels back. Ace's television slowly traveled backwards as he pointed the remote at the screen. Five stations later, he could not believe his eyes. He increased the volume on the television and his mouth fell open at the photo on the television screen.

"Blytheville Police Department have no leads as to the whereabouts of the suspects or the escapees. We'll have more as this horrendous story unfolds.

"What the fuck," Ace cursed as he switched to another channel station. He tuned just in time to catch the beginning of the story. Ace's head was in a whirlwind. He rubbed his eyes and shook his head to make sure he wasn't dreaming. He did not want to believe what his eyes had just witnessed nor what his ears just heard.

"This shit keeps getting better and better." He shook his head and let out an insane laughter.

Beads of perspiration began to form on his forehead and his palms started to itch. A sense of fear swept through Ace for a split second.

"Damn," he cursed as he retrieved his cell phone. Just as he was about to search for the intended phone number in his phone, he heard a loud noise. Without hesitation, he reached over and grabbed his .357 snub nose revolver handgun he had laid alongside the mattress he laid on. A sharp pain jolted through his entire body due to how swiftly he had moved to obtain the handgun, but that didn't matter to him. The only thing that mattered now was survival. He wondered how they had found him and who "they" were. There were only two people who knew about his hole-in-the-wall spot. One, his friend Moe, and the other: Big Face, the one person he knew could help him and would never betray him. He had already made up his mind that if it were the fed or police, he was not going back to federal prison, he told himself. He made up his mind long ago that he would be carried by six rather than judged by twelve. Ace grabbed hold of his injured shoulder and rose up. He clenched his teeth to endure the pain. He steadily made his way over towards the back door of the basement. At that moment he heard another sound, only this time it was a much louder sound than the first one. He could tell they were footsteps. One set of footsteps. At that point, he knew it could not have been the authorities. He was sure they wouldn't have come alone and would have already busted the upstairs door down and bum-rushed him. Ace could feel his heart beating fast against his chest at a rapid pace as the realization of who it could be had dawned on him. How could it be? He thought to himself. It can't be. He shook his head at the strong possibility.

Then out of nowhere Diamond answered his question. *Then his question was answered.* Ace heard a female voice from behind him. It was a voice he thought he'd never hear again.

"Payback time, mutha'fucka bitch!"

Not wanting to go out like a bitch, Ace wasted no time and sprung into action. He spun around quicker than Prince in the *Purple Rain* video and squeezed the trigger of his revolver until he heard the clicking sound of an empty pistol. His eyes widened at the sight of the figure, which was not just mere inches away from him.

"You thought I wasn't comin' for you?" Her voice echoed in the distance as she raised her barrel upward to his temple.

Ace couldn't bring himself to utter a word. He knew he had been caught slipping, literally, with his pants down. All Ace could do was smile. He closed his eyes, as he felt the cold steel pressed against his dome. Diamond's cannon gun roared just seconds before the bullet exited the chamber.

The sound of the shot caused Ace to jump out of his sleep. He was sweating profusely. Despite the fact that he now realized he was having the same recurring nightmare, instantly he reached for his gun and bounced up. He wondered how long he had been asleep as he looked at the alarm clock in the corner. Only two hours had passed, he noticed, since he had placed his call. They had told him the faster they could get to him was in three hours. Ace located the remote to the television to lower the volume. He noticed the wet stains that outlined his head on the soft pillow and where his body laid along with the additional bloodstain. He lugged himself to the bathroom and flicked on the light. He turned on the faucet and cupped his hand to quench his thirst, then splashed the cold water onto his face. He stared in the mirror. He almost didn't recognize himself. His eyes were bloodshot, his skin coloration seemed dull, and his once puffy face from good living seemed to have deflated somewhat. Ace shook his head and lowered it. What a difference a week could make, he thought to himself. Just a week ago, he was on top, living the good life. Now, he was in a filthy hole of a basement like Saddam Hussein, with nothing, fighting and running for his dear life. The more he thought about it, the angrier he became. There was only one person to blame, he reasoned with himself. Ace banged his fist on the porcelain sink. He knew the only way now for him to get back everything and then some was to restore his health and take action. Ace raised his head and took one last look at the mirror. He didn't know whether he wanted to laugh or cry. Instead, a psychotic grimace appeared across his face. He knew there was only one thing left to do if he wanted to make it out of his situation in one piece.

"I must find this bitch before she finds me!" he said out loud before dousing a handful of water in his face for a second time.

Diamond peered out of the rearview mirror of her pearl white Cadillac Escalade for the third time as she drove down the road. She stroked the handle of her black nine millimeter Beretta, which rested between her legs, as she studied the dark colored vehicle trailing three cars lengths behind her.

"I hope I don't have to put you to work today," she referenced aloud to her pistol. Hopefully, she was just overreacting and the blunt of exotic she, Angel, and Raven had smoked before she left had her paranoid like hell. Ever since she had dropped her aunt and uncle off the money for the monthly rent, she jumped on the road on a mission. Diamond felt somebody was following her. Since they had been in Arkansas, they had tried to keep the lowest profile they possibly could and only did business with a small circle of people they had met through one of her male cuz. It was not easy, especially since they had the best kilos of cocaine prices from around the world. She wondered who could be tailing her, knowing what type of heat came with the drug game. She knew it could only be one of two people, the police or stick up boys in the hood. No matter who it was though, Diamond made up her mind she was not going back to Yazoo Mississippi federal prison. Nor was she going out without a fight. She cursed herself for leaving her cell phone back at the house.

Junebug had emphasized on more than one occasion that none of them should ever leave out of the house without their phones in case of an emergency, but she was speeding and rushed out without thought. Now here, it was her carelessness that could be the cause of her losing her freedom or her life. At that moment, Diamond knew the true meaning of *a hard head makes a soft behind*. She grimaced as the car sped up and closed in the gap between them. "Fuck," Diamond mumbled under her breath

It was now only a car length behind her SUV. The gold Honda emblem of the red car illuminated in Diamond's rearview. She was seeing all kinds of crazy colors. Diamond noticed two bodies in the front seat of the vehicle but between the tint on the top of the front windshield and the glare from the beaming southern sun, it made it difficult for her to get a good look at the occupants. Diamond's speedometer read: 59 miles per hour. Despite the speed limit being 55mph, she accelerated until the needle surpassed 65 mph. The vehicle behind her followed suit in speed. "Okay, you wanna play, mutha'fuckas." She sat erect in her vehicle. She could feel her adrenaline pumping. Diamond increased the volume of her Gucci Mane song on the steering wheel. With her turn coming up soon, she knew it was now or never. There was no way she was going to lead whoever was following her to her hood. Diamond removed the safety on her weapon and unlocked the Escalade doors. As she reached the two-way intersection, she began to slow her speed. Rather than making her normal right, she hooked a left. By now, she had her gun tightly gripped in her right hand ready for whatever was about to go down. She wasted no time pulling off to the side of the road. She placed one hand on the SUV's door handle and the other on the trigger of her weapon. Despite the chill from the air conditioner, sweat trickled down the side of Diamond's face. This is it, she thought, as she waited for the car's next move. To her surprise, the red Honda kept straight. She watched as the car cruised by the intersection. Within seconds, it disappeared into the distance. She wiped the remaining perspiration that had formed on her forehead with the palm of her hand. "Damn, I need to stop smokin' that shit." She laughed out loud. "Sorry, girl, false alarm!" she told her gun. She kissed the side of her gun before she slipped it back between her legs, then busted a U-turn in the middle of the road.

Chapter 15

"Nigga, why the hell you didn't turn behind that bitch?" Butch shouted at his partner, Fred.

"For what?" Fred answered. "You ain't see that her fuckin' ass was on to us? Would you had been the one to tell big bruh if we would've fucked this up?" He followed up with a question.

Butch let out a gust of hot air in frustration.

"I'm getting tired of all this waiting shit. We should've just grabbed that bitch back in Thug Town and forced her to tell us where all that dope at. Instead, we ridin' around following muthafuckas."

Fred peered over at his partner. He knew how impatient Butch could be at times. It was the same lack of patience that had gotten them caught on stealing charges and sent them to the detention center when they were young. They were known for stealing shit, to be honest. The very same reacting-without-thinking-first mentality that had nearly gotten them killed at a juke joint in Blytheville. They were only 19 years old when he had overestimated them, which had landed them both in the county jail for several months and then to prison years ago.

No matter what the case, Fred continued to take the bitter with the sweet. The two of them had a history and the good outweighed the bad. There were times when Fred had put them in situations or predicaments that would have caused them to lose their freedom or their life. Butch had never complained about it. They were crime partners and Fred knew his partner always had his back. The two were friends and all the others had never seen this coming. Aside from Butch being short, brown-skinned and stocky he was a killer on sight. Fred was black, tall and slim, yet the two men had a lot in common.

They were both an only child and had grown up together in Blytheville in the small government housing projects. They had took it to the streets and started doing stick-ups and other petty jobs. Since they were young, they had to find, as a means of survival, a way to cope after Fred's mother was stabbed to death by one of her jealous lovers. Neither of the two knew their fathers, and the rest of their family didn't want anything to do with them. It was actually Fred's idea to start robbing and stealing. Butch went along with the idea, no question asked. Both their bond and trust in one another was unbreakable.

"Man, I knew I should've drove," Butch shouted.

Fred shook his head as he anticipated his friend's next words. He had heard them so many times in similar situations that he could just about recite them himself. "I would've run that bitch off the road and shoved 'ole Bessy in her mouth and made her tell me what we needed to know," Butch said, referring to his 44 revolver.

Fred mocked Butch under his breath nearly verbatim until he had ended his famous speech.

"What if she wouldn't have talked?" Fred posed the question as he drove. He always got a kick out of his partner's responses whenever he posed the question.

"Then ole Bessy would've done the talking for her city slickin' ass!" Butch kissed the side of his revolver. "Ain't that right, girl?" He addressed his gun.

"Then we would've been right back to square one and you would've had some explaining to do." Fred smiled at him as he searched for a comeback.

"Well, your ass got some explaining to do now since you let that bitch get away."

"I guess," Fred shrugged as he made his way back to Gosnell Arkansas. "I'm going to warn you now. I'm not afraid to die and hope you not neither in these streets. Therefore, I am definitely not afraid to kill a muthafucka. If the streets want to do business, then they do it with me as they have been doing it or they can suck my dick. Either way, a nigga good."

Chapter 16

Mustafa staggered out of the Holiday Inn hotel, intoxicated by a cocktail of exotic drugs. He wore so much jewelry that when he walked he made loud metallic clinging sounds. Animated, he wobbled over to the wall and grabbed it as if he were trying to stop the building from falling. The front of his *True Religion* pants were soiled with a large piss stain that ran the length of his left pant leg. That night, he was faced with one of the biggest dilemmas of the day— should he take his dick out and piss right there in front of the hotel or vomit first.

With his world spinning, his bodily functions didn't give him a chance to decide. With his dick in his right hand, he began to vomit and urinate uncontrollably. It truly was a sight to behold.

Afterwards, with his mouth ringed with vomit, he staggered away while trying to place his big dick back into his jeans. He looked up, and through bleary eyes, he saw Trina floating toward him. He tried to wipe his mouth with his shirt sleeve and smile. Even in the dim light, he could still make out the symmetry of her sexy body. He staggered slightly in a failed attempt to gain his equilibrium.

"Heyyy, honey!" Trina caroled seductively in a breathy voice as she walked up to him, enrapturing him with the wiles of her charm.

"Damn … you the sexy broad round town … I mean … ahh … uhh," Mustafa stammered as he recalled seeing her.

His mouth was still partially ringed with vomit. Everything was still spinning, but starting to slow down pace. He let go of the wall, his legs wobbling unsteadily like a child just learning to walk. Trina came closer. He reached out and fondled one of her nice breasts. She rewarded him with a laugh as jubilant as a young schoolkid on her first date. She furtively glanced over her shoulder at Mack hunched low in the car watching her every move.

"Babe girl, you wanna come inside and chill? A player got everything you might need to make your life complete. You like to smoke weed? I got … I got …" Drunk, Mustafa lost his train of thought at the moment as he snatched his head. "I got what you need," he said, causing her to tentatively take a step back.

Shit! His breath smells just like cat shit, she thought as she noticed a puddle of vomit on the ground in front of him. It took everything in her power not to frown as he once again caressed her breasts. Talk about being an actress, she deserved all the Oscar that can be won.

"I would love to come inside," she drawled. "You still want me to suck that small dick?" She smiled. She licked her sexy lips and reached down to rub his dick. As she did that, she felt a wet spot. *Nasty bitch*, she thought to herself as she removed her hand and placed it on her shirt, slyly wiping her small hand.

"Big boy, why don't you walk me to my car first, to lock it up … tight," she cajoled, puckering her luscious lips, showing him one of her cum faces.

"Wha … wha … where you parked at, baby girl?" Mustafa asked.

She laughed innocently, taking his hand and walking him toward Mack in the parked car. He staggered a few steps and suddenly stopped in his tracks. His eyes popped open as if he'd seen a ghost. He stared at something in the distance. Whatever it was spooked him, causing him to sober up quickly.

"Nawl, honey. I just saw something across the street. A light went on in that van."

He squinted as if trying to focus in his inebriated fog. Mustafa pulled away from her hand and started to back pedal out of her grasp.

Not again, Trina thought as she remembered the scene back at the strip club. How mad Mack was with her for letting him get away.

Think fast! Think fast! Trick-ass nigga getting away! her mind churned. She reached into her purse and pulled out an elegant nickel-plated .357 Derringer pistol. It was the size of a Bic lighter, but powerful enough to drop an elephant on his ass.

"Take another step, bitch-ass-nigga, and Imma blow your whole fuckin' head off. Now try me!" she said coldly between clenched teeth. Her face was a mask of deadly intent.

For some reason, in her mind, everything moved in slow motion, surreal motion. A lavender sky was starting to peek over the pitch-black horizon as dawn, like a dirty sheet on the canvas of the night, exposed the good, the bad and the ugly. In the distance, birds were starting to chirp loud, summoning morning.

"Ebony, Ebony, don't shoot me!" he begged.

They were standing only inches apart. A lone car passed, and its luminous headlights traced their bodies, stalled in the night. The air suddenly turned cool with the imminent threat of death. Sweat gleamed on Mustafa's forehead as he stood panic-stricken, overcome with fear. Ebony could tell he was thinking about bolting. There was no doubt whatsoever in her mind—if Mustafa tried to get away, she would kill him.

The lobby doors opened and out walked Mustafa's bodyguard. The man was huge. He stood about six feet, eight inches, three hundred and something pounds. He had broad shoulders like a mountain. The man's name was Consequence. He was an ex-convict and a well-known killer.

As soon as Con got out the joint, Mustafa gave him a job as head of Lilly Street Mafia security. Next to Con stood Ice Man, who was slightly built, with a baby face and long eyelashes. He resembled the rapper Gucci Mane. Both men were strapped with guns.

"Hey, man! What the fuck is going on out here?" Con asked suspiciously as he took a step closer.

His deep, throaty baritone voice seemed to resonate with the timbre of a man that commanded authority.

Playfully, Trina laughed and hugged Mustafa as she placed the barrel of the gun against his rib cage and whispered in his ear as Con approached, "Tell them you'll be inside in a second."

"I'ma … I'ma … I'ma be inside in a second," the frightened man said, raising his voice.

"Bitch ass nigga, you know you got on too much ice," Con warned as he stepped closer. He was only a few feet from Trina now. "Come on, man, let's go."

"You finna be shittin' in a plastic bag, rollin' around in a wheelchair," Trina whispered in Mustafa's ear, feeling Con's presence was too damn close. She pushed the gun harder against his ribs.

"Man! I told cha, I'm fuckin coming! Leave me the fuck alone!" Mustafa yelled at his bodyguard, causing him to exchange looks with Ice Man.

They both shrugged as if to say, "Fuck him, let him have his way, the bitch" as they walked away.

Trina could feel Mustafa's arms shaking like leaves on an apple tree.

"Ebony don't kill me," Mustafa pleaded.

"Shut up, nigga!" she said as she peeked over in Mack's direction, huddled in the car.

Just then, a weary crackhead prostitute walked up. She was dressed in raggedy clothes—a pair of jeans that looked like they had not been washed in days, sneakers and a once-white halter top that was now gray. Her eyes continued to dart suspiciously back and forth across the street as she smacked her lips as if she had just bitten into a sour lemon or apple candy.

She jerked her long neck, snaking it from side to side, her hand poised hyperactively on her body as she patted her foot on the concrete. On a crackhead's impulse, her eyes began to search the ground where she had lost her rock the other night.

Her foot did a casual sweep of the pavement as she made a face twisting her lips as she said matter-of-factly: "Girlfriend, I think that's the law across the street parked in that van."

Hearing that caused Mustafa's body to flinch uncontrollably.

"Shit!" Trina muttered as she glanced over at the white van.

Why didn't I recognize it earlier? she thought.

"Imma scream if you don't let me go," Mustafa whimpered.

Something about hearing the word "police" had emboldened him.

"Nigga, you stunt if you wanna, and I'ma leave your punk ass slumped right here with a hole in your chest!" Trina hissed as she cocked the gun and pressed it harder against his ribs.

Mustafa was standing on the balls of his feet as if that would ease the explosion if the gun went off, shattering his rib cage and blowing his whole back out.

The prostitute continued to look back and forth in all directions, including the ground, akin to a junkie's perpetual paranoia.

Once again Trina glanced over at the car with Mack in it and then looked at the undercover police van.

"Ain't this about a bitch!"

***

145

"Unit 2 to Captain Snow . . ."

"Go ahead, this is Captain Snow," an authoritative voice returned over the sporadic cracking of the police radio.

"Lieutenant Brown is trying to reach you on the phone."

Snow turned on his cell phone and it rang instantly. The Lieutenant spoke urgently. "The suspect and his entourage have just turned off Maple Avenue onto Cherry Avenue. They're at the Holiday Inn."

"You're in fuckin' Gosnell Arkansas now?" Captain Snow shrieked over the phone, thinking about the friction it would cause with the 62nd Windwood. They already had a bad rivalry, and this would only make things worse.

"I want you and the rest of the team to steer clear of the suspect until I get there and give the order to take his black ass down," Captain barked over the phone.

"Captain."

"What?" Snow answered brusquely.

"Sir, there appears to be a black Range Rover with a black female driving. There is also another individual in the car that we can't seem to make out. They have been trailing the suspect all night long. The car is now illegally parked in front of the Holiday Inn. How shall we proceed?"

"Leave the car alone. We don't want to risk tipping off the 62nd that we're on their turf about to make a major bust. They're probably harmless groupies. Tell your team to hang tight. I'm on my way." Snow hung up the phone and made a U-turn in the middle of the street.

As he drove, his mind went over every detail as it related to how he was going to make the bust. Mustafa was actually out of Snow's jurisdiction, but since his department had tailed him from Blytheville Arkansas to Osceola Arkansas, in violation of possession of drugs and guns, the arrest was going to be perfectly legal. Now all Snow had to do was plant the dope.

The good thing about what he was doing was that the Mayor himself was behind the special task force to arrest as many niggas as they could, and so far, so good. His department had been having a field day. The only thing that kept Mustafa on the streets for so long was the fact that he was a low-key person with several businesses.

Mustafa had switched the game from hustler to entrepreneur in the blink of an eye. But now felt he was invincible and refused to provide Snow with any information because he wasn't a snitch. Snow hated that he didn't bust Mustafa earlier. Now he was selling dope everywhere just like all the cartels in the world.

This fueled Snow even more as his nondescript Chevy sliced through the night. What really pissed him off was to see a black man making so much damn money, legally. They were becoming a threat. Hell, the Lilly Street Mafia, one of the hottest blocks, had just bought a mansion with twenty-one rooms, a bowling alley, basketball court inside, and a large movie theater. Another was a partial owner of a soccer team. It was becoming a trend.

"How do they do it?" he pondered.

His knuckles were white as he tightly held onto the steering wheel as the car reached speeds of over a hundred miles per hour. He was consumed with the anticipation of the bust. He felt the adrenaline of a policeman's head rush—the set-up, the chase, the capture and then arrest. Just the thought of it gave him an erection. He would teach the fucker who he was playing with.

Besides, Snow wanted to please the Mayor. He was already told to treat all niggas as potential drug dealers until proven differently. Now, all he had to do was follow the first law of police work—if there isn't a crime, invent one.

Captain Snow made the excursion to the location in 20 minutes flat. Light out, he cruised past the *Cream Castle* food restaurant where a few prostitutes loitered.

Unbeknownst to him, somewhere, somehow, in the hub of this naked city, the streets were watching, waiting, listening. Snow eased, a pitbull dog barked in the distance.

A crescent moon, embellished with stars, hung from the night sky like a lucid scratch on the underbelly of the black canvas of the night.

A weary prostitute ambled by. The woman took one look at the supposed undercover law and decided he damn sure was not a trick. She took off walking fast, looking over her shoulder as if to make sure the cop made no attempt to tackle her.

The night air felt crisp and cool against Snow's pale skin as he walked toward the surveillance van. He realized that he was starting to sweat under his Polo cotton shirt, causing it to stick to his bare skin like glue on paper.

The foul odor of rotten garbage mixed with air pollution only seemed to enhance the moment. Eyes alert, he could feel his senses tingling as he felt for the ounce of meth he had in his pocket. He intended to plant the dope on Mustafa.

Lieutenant Brown opened the van door. Snow grunted as he squatted, struggling to get in. The twenty-four pounds he had picked up over the last few years were starting to take their toll on him. There were five other undercover officers in the cramped van.

"Captain, I just received word from the 62nd. They want to know what we're doing on their turf. They're asking us to back off and let them handle the arrest."

"Handle my ass! I'm in command here. My authority comes all the way from the Mayor's office," Snow screeched. He thought about the dope in his pocket intended for Mustafa.

"Tell whomever it is that I said to fuck him and his bitch ass mother to death!"

"Man, damn!" one of the black undercover officers lamented as he looked through the night vision binoculars.

Snow snatched the binoculars and peered out the window. As he bent down, he accidentally hit a switch, causing the inside of the van to light up.

Chapter 17

Trina stood in front of the hotel paralyzed with fear as she held the gun against Mustafa's ribs. The prostitute had just warned her that the police were parked across the street in the van.

Mack had spied everything from the confines of the car, but he had no idea that the police were parked nearby watching them.

Don't panic, Trina thought as her mind frantically searched for a way out, but it was for Mack. They both didn't have to go to prison if she could help it. She fully intended to save him by any means necessary. Suddenly, she had an idea.

"Give her all your money," Trina ordered, shoving the gun handle against his ribs.

"What?" Mustafa asked.

"Nigga, you heard me!" Trina raised her voice.

The prostitute continued to look on. Four people walked out of the large hotel, a woman and three men. The woman saw what was going on, but played it off as she quickened her pace and nudged one of her partners. They saw, but didn't see. In the real world of the ghetto, a hero gets punished, sometimes even killed, for interfering in other people's business.

The foursome passed on their way to the parking lot.

Mustafa's hands were shaking so bad when he handed the prostitute the wad of money that the diamond platinum bracelets on his arms chimed like bells. He gave the junkie a little over six thousand dollars.

"Listen, you got a family?" Trina asked the hooker.

"Yeah, I got a nine-year-old son," the junkie replied, eyes as big as silver dollars as she licked her dry lips.

"I have a family too," Trina said as she spied the van across the street. That's my family parked in that car across the street over there." Trina pointed with a nod of her head. "I want you to promise me that you'll take the money and do something for your boy. But first I want you to walk over there and tell that nigga parked in the car . . . tell him to go. Tell him the police are watching us, like a set-up. "Tell him the spot is hot. Tell him . . ." Trina's voice cracked, "Tell him I love him."

Why Trina didn't walk away and let Mustafa go was a mystery. It was as if she couldn't stop, not even if she wanted to. Since Mack had gone away, robbery was what her body needed to feel of command over another's soul. Mustafa was the fix for her addiction.

Hauntingly, she was often reminded of a story she had watched as a small kid on television, on PBS. It was a horrific story about how African monkeys are hunted, trapped and killed. The hunter merely places a shiny object inside a cage and the monkey reaches inside the cage to grab the shiny object. It's too big to get out of the narrow bars of the cage, and when the hunters come to trap him, even at the risk of his own life, the monkey is too dumb to let go, and is ultimately killed for refusing to let go.

Like the monkey, Trina refused to let go, and she knew someday it would cost her her life.

She spun Mustafa around and made mad laughter like the two of them were lovebirds having a friendly frolic. She walked him toward the parking garage. There, she intended to strip him down like a stolen car at the chop shop.

Inside the dark garage, the stench of piss was strong. As she continued to walk him like a dog in the dim light, her mind raced.

How was she going to pull this shit off? The entire time, he whimpered and pleaded for his life. Suddenly, up ahead, car lights flashed and tires screeched.

Startled, she braced herself as she held Mustafa by his shirt, leveling the gun at his kidneys. The car continued to accelerate toward her, its headlights engulfing them like deer standing in the middle of the street.

"Police! Police!"

Trina feared for her life.

The car came to a screeching halt only inches in front of them. Mack jumped out wearing a black ski mask and a black bullet-proof vest.

He rushed over to her and pointed the AK-47 at Mustafa's head. "Nigga, I should kill you." For the second time that day, he pissed in his pants.

A few yards away a woman screamed loudly. It was the same bitch that had passed Trina earlier with her companions. They were about to enter a cream colored Benz. The woman continued to scream. Mack rushed over to her and slapped her upside the head with the bottom of his gun. Silence. She dropped like a sack of rocks as her companions grimaced in horror.

"Gimme your car keys and wallets, bitch!" Mack commanded. His voice echoed.

Mack was moving fast as Trina looked on. "Remember, I got your IDs, so I know how to find you. Lie on the ground and be quiet until I tell you to talk."

Both men obeyed and lay down on the pissy concrete. Mack quickly moved to the back of the Benz, opening the trunk with the car keys. He pointed the gun at Mustafa, waving for Trina to come on.

He was moving too slow, so she shoved him so hard his glasses fell off and he nearly fell as he stumbled. Trina marched him over to the open trunk.

"Girl, what the fuck you tryna do? You fuckin' death struck or something?" Mack said as he hit Mustafa across the head with his gun. As Mustafa fell, Trina tried to grab him by his shirts, but it tore in half. Mustafa hit his forehead on the concrete with a thud.

Moving swiftly, together they hoisted his body into the trunk as they both heard the blare of police sirens. Alarmed, they looked at each other. Mack threw her the car keys. "It's on you, sweetie. If they open the trunk I'm comin' out blastin." He dived into the trunk next to the unconscious Mustafa.

Trina slammed the trunk closed, ran and jumped into the front seat. Placing the key in the ignition, she took a deep breath in an attempt to calm her nerves. She pulled off and headed toward the exit.

In front of her, lights blared as sirens shrilled in her ears. Up ahead a caravan of law cars raced toward them. *It ain't gonna fuckin' go down like this*, she thought as her heart pounded so hard in her chest that it felt like it was going to explode.

A police car pulled in front of her, blocking her path. Trina clinched the gun in her hand as she thought about Mustafa in the trunk. She was thinking about going out like "Set It Off." Two police officers hopped out of their cars with guns drawn, aimed at her head. "Get out the car now! Get out of the car, now!" One officer was Asian, the other black.

Trina palmed the small gun in her hand. Her life flashed before her eyes, the monkey that couldn't let go. Her mind churned, *Think fast! Think fast!*

"Noooo! Nooo!" she cried hysterically.

"There's a masked gunman back there! He tried to kidnap me! He already has one hostage back there with him." She pointed with her hand while the other clasped the gun between her legs as she continued to cry the way only a black woman could to save her man and herself. She manufactured an ocean of tears, with a "please help me, woman in distress" face to match. Somehow, she was able to melt the heart of the Asian cop, but the nigga cop looked at her crazy.

The Asian cop looked behind Trina to the other end of the parking garage as he spoke. "I want you to drive out of here to safety and park your car on the side of the building in the alleyway. I'll send an officer to get a description of the gunman."

Trina nodded as she listened to the police giving her orders. A dry lump formed in her throat as she swallowed. "Okay," she muttered as she listened to the cop call for more backup on his radio. He requested for the SWAT team. She did as instructed, and drove slowly through the throngs of police cars and flashing lights, all the while unconscious of the fact that she was holding her breath and praying to God that she thought never listening to her.

***

"What the hell is going on?" Snow shrieked, his face flustered as she watched from the concealment of the van.

The beautiful black girl and Mustafa flirted and touched on each other. The two men walked out. There was an exchange of words. The two men left, few other people passed and suddenly the crackhead that Snow had seen earlier was talking to the couple and the fine black chick walked Mustafa to the parking garage.

She's probably going to give him some head, Snow thought.

Moments later the car followed the chick into the garage. The next thing Snow knew, all hell broke loose. A woman's scream echoed from the garage and police came from everywhere.

"What the hell the 62nd police department doing there?" The scene was pure madness. The streets were cluttered with police cars from all positions.

Snow watched the Range Rover slowly drive out of the garage and weave through the congested streets.

"Sir, that's the 62nd Police Department," an officer said to his Captain.

"Thought I gave you orders to tell them to back the fuck off!" Snow spat angrily.

"I did," the officer barked back, making a face as he scurried to get out of the van.

"Motherfucking bureaucratic bullshit!" Snow yelled as he got out of the van and stormed over to the handsomely dressed, plain-clothes officer who had just arrived on the scene and was giving orders.

"Who's in fucking charge here?" Snow huffed.

"I am," the handsome black man said as he turned to meet the other man's stare. "And you've just fucked up for not getting permission from 62nd Street."

"Fuck 62nd buddy, and you with it. Who the hell are you?"

"Lieutenant Small." He pulled out his badge.

"Well, by the time I'm finished with you, you'll be LT. Dick, working somewhere in Mexico!"

Just then, the police radio crackled to life. Lieutenant Small signaled for one of his men to pass him their radio. "Lt. Small, go ahead."

"There are two males and an unconscious female in here," the voice on the other end replied urgently. "One of the males said an armed gunman hit his girl upside the head and stole their car. The other male claims he doesn't remember what went down. Be advised, a woman and a man were seen placing an individual in the trunk of a stolen Benz. These individuals are to be considered armed and dangerous."

Lieutenant Small looked over at Captain Snow as the irate man kicked the side of the car. The voice on the other end of the radio continued, "One of the suspects, the woman, talked her way past a couple of officers. She's driving the Benz. There is also an abandoned black Range Rover."

"Black Range Rover?" Snow retorted as his eyebrows shot up as he thought about the girl.

She wasn't a groupie, he thought. He now realized she was part of some elaborate robbery scheme. He looked up to see the Benz turning the corner.

"There they go!" he shouted.

As Trina slowly drove away with her human cargo in the trunk, she had no idea just how bad her day was going to get.

Chapter 18

Turning his attention back to the block, Junebug thought about the promise he had solemnly made to all his homies in the joint, his heroes, the players that stood up like men and did their time giving the ultimate sacrifice, their lives, rather than betray the street code of ethics. Men knew that snitching on a man was no different than committing genocide because you're not just killing the man, you're killing the family, too. Somebody's father, son, brother, or husband.

As Junebug looked down at Moe, he knew that he must be made an example of, but he was also smart enough to realize that his feelings were not much involved. Moe had done more damage to Junebug than he should have, but still the dying man refused to tell him where the money was stashed. Maybe Moe didn't have the money after all, but Moe knew that would be going against the grain or street code.

All real hustlers had a stash spot. Even when they do get legit, it's in their DNA — you never know when it'll be time to get little around this bitch.

The problem was: making them talk. Junebug had long reasoned that was the whole purpose behind kidnapping. Ironically, in a world where dissemination of information was prevalent, kidnapping crossed all barriers and more. Men, women, children of all races were fair game for the fine art of abduction.

Frustrated, Junebug turned the handle on the vice, tightening it on Moe's skull, causing him to scream loud enough to wake the dead; if not the dead, the hood for sure. The pain was so excruciating that Moe almost welcomed death; that's some crazy shit.

Once again, Junebug thought: *Why won't this nigga tell where that bag of money at?*

Junebug had damn near busted Moe's skull, and he had lost a lot of blood. He had recalled reading literature somewhere dealing with a Mexican technique of torture. It involved teeth and the very sensitive nerves at the root of each tooth that are connected to the brain. Bug knew that he had to think of something fast.

At the end of the workstation was a pair of old rusty pliers. He reached over and picked them up. Taking a long day off the blunt, he looked down at Moe as thick smoke smoldered, curling out of his big nose.

Junebug said mildly, "Open your mouth." Moe's one good eye stretched as wide as "Pinky" pussy and a gold coin as he realized what Junebug intended to do with the pliers. "Pinky The Pornstar has a big pussy. Can you imagine how wide his mouth is opening?"

"Ahh, uhm," Moe mumbled, clamping his bruised lips shut tightly, making a face to show he refused to open his big mouth.

Junebug turned the handle to the jaws of the vice on Moe's head, causing him to open his mouth to scream. Junebug shoved the pliers inside his mouth, grabbing teeth and gums, twisting and pulling a crunching sound of teeth being torn away violently from the root.

"Nigga, where dat cheese at?" Junebug yelled as he tethered on the ball of his toes, yanking and pulling. Moe experienced more pain than he had ever felt race through his small brain.

Finally, Junebug yanked out three teeth matted with gory, blood-dripping gums that resembled a chunk of steak meat.

He chimed as he dropped the teeth on the floor, wiped his hands on his pants leg and prepared to go back into Moe's mouth. Moe choked and gagged as blood poured from his mouth like a broken water fountain. His lips moved, but no words came out. He was trying to speak as he drifted in and out of consciousness. He knew that sleep was the cousin's death.

"Daddy's . . . crib . . ." Moe muttered as he dreamed of his body at peace in a gold closed casket. He welcomed it.

"Nigga, what did you say?" Junebug asked, leaning over, placing his ear near Moe's lips.

No answer.

Junebug reached for the bloody pliers again, determined to make him talk.

"Stop! Stop!" Ebony hollered. She was terrified as she wobbled while holding her stomach. "Baby, I think he's tryna tell you something." Remember this was the same woman talking that has kids by Junebug brother. It's ashamed she was fucking the other brother.

"Well, I'm glad you finally woke the hell up," Bug said sarcastically as he glared at her. She ignored him as she forced her eyes away from the horrific sight of Moe's bloodied body.

Damn, how much pain can one man take? His face was barely recognizable as blood poured from both his mouth and eye. The right side of his chest was now caved in from where Junebug had beaten him with a house brick. Simply said, it was just too much for her to bear.

"The money … is … at my … daddy's … crib," Moe whispered in a hoarse voice. The one secret that every hustler knew he was supposed to take to his grave. Jeopardizing the life of his family, Moe began to cough and spasm. He was choking on his own blood. Ebony frowned as she felt her knees about to buckle, and she held onto the nearby table for support.

"That's more like it, nigga," Junebug said with a smirk as he took a long pull of the blunt, rubbing his hands together anxiously.

It suddenly dawned on him why Moe had refused to tell where the money was — a man's love for his family. Being the snake that he was, Moe had told on him, too, with no remorse.

To Ebony, her brief exposure to the other side of the life of a real gangsta bitch was something she would never forget. In the years to come, she would adopt Junebug's style of torture, just like she had been emulating everything else about Peanut. However, what she didn't know was, under the dirty apple standards of kidnapping and holding them for ransom policy, Junebug's demonstration of torture to make them tell was the soft version. Normally, body parts were sent to the family members as evidence that they were dead serious about their cash. So far, Junebug had not cut off any body parts, at least not yet.

Moe spilled his little guts like he was on *The First 48* crime scenes. He told Junebug about the money he had stashed at his parents' house. It was a little over three million dollars in cash. Moe pleaded the best he could for Junebug not to kill his family and kids.

Junebug assured him he wouldn't under one condition — Moe had to get on the phone and tell his family that a woman was coming over to get the money to buy a home. Moe agreed. He made the phone call on one of the many cellular phones that Bug had just for the occasion. The phone was stolen, so it couldn't be traced back to the caller. Junebug kept prepaid phones for his drug business.

To all their amazement, Moe was able to speak to his daddy. Instantly his father knew something was mad wrong as his son gave him instructions to give the three duffel bags of money that were stashed inside the basement to a woman that was coming to retrieve them. The entire time he spoke, his daddy's intuition kicked in and like most parents with a son in the dope game — they knew the territory of the game. His mother was living proof of that. Their son had taken them out of the ghetto and placed them in a big mansion on the hill in the suburbs of Blytheville Arkansas. His son drove a new model Benz. He knew the risk of his son's lifestyle were high, but what he didn't know, as he held the phone with his hands trembling, was that it would be his last time ever speaking to his oldest kid.

Ebony put on a disguise – a black wig, dark Chanel shades and a St. Louis baseball cap on and walked up the street to catch a local cab to grab the money. One thing for certain, Moe's parents would never call the law unless they was sure that their son was in harm's way.

With the help of the local cab driver, Ebony made it to the house. When Moe's father asked about his son before he gave her the money with tears in his eyes Ebony could not dare to look the man in his face as her mind flashed back to several horrific scenes when she went to jail and sold all her material things to stay free. Junebug standing over Moe holding a kitchen bloodied six-inch knife. *Imma dress your punk-ass-up and send you back home to your family in a woody pine box*, she remembers him saying.

"Yes, daddy, your son will be back home soon. He just had too much to drink, and told me to come," Ebony lied, not bothering to look the older man in the eyes.

After she had picked up the money, everything went as planned. Now came the really hard part—take over the town once again but with a different man.

Junebug was going to have to recruit Ebony one last time for the most dangerous task of all. As you can see, everybody is fucking the same woman at some point of time in the dope game.

Junebug contemplated his plans as Moe lay on the table looking like a human science nigga project about to go bad. His lips moved, gurgling blood, as he struggled to speak. Junebug bent down, nearly placing his eye to his mouth.

"Don't … leave … me … like this … kill … me … nigga …" Moe pleaded plaintively in a dry hoarse voice as blood dripped from his ears.

The claw-like clamps of the vice grip on his head were so tight it was slowly crushing his skull. As Moe begged to be killed, Junebug furtively nodded with sympathy as he reached down to the floor, retrieving a pair of shears used in lawn maintenance. The sharp instrument was for cutting through thick bushes, but Junebug had another purpose in mind.

"Imma need one more thing from you," Junebug said matter-of-factly, ignoring Moe's pleas for death. "I want your lyin'-ass tongue and head for a kind of souvenir, a special memento to send to the good Mayor of Blytheville and the police chief. Especially the rest of them hot-ass-nigga to let them know that us real gangstas is still runnin' shit."

"You … fuckkin' crazy, nigga!" Moe said between short breaths.

"I know, I know," Junebug said in a singsong voice, "and that's why I promise you, Imma send a lot of niggas to join you."

With that, Junebug turned the vice, causing Moe to open his mouth for the last time. He violently shoved the shears into Moe's mouth in order to cut his tongue out. Afterward, tired and bloody, Junebug needed a handsaw and some garbage bags. He was determined to make a grand statement: "Keep your fucking mouth shut," as he cut his head off.

Chapter 19

Gigi got the moniker because she dominated many cities' criminal world for many decades. Her name may not resonate with today's young gang bangers in the hood. Consequence and Justice had a lot of respect for her. She was the only person they could trust to handle business without a second guest. Con loved that about her to the fullest. The laws picked her up at least 40 times on 75 different charges, as her drug business and gambling business made her a familiar figure to law enforcement.

Yet, despite her legal problems, she did not keep a low profile. For instance, she was known to give big parties in Memphis Tenn., where she regularly put out bowls of cocaine and weed for her special guests.

She decided that she would make a lot of money in life and she was not going to be particular in how she did it. She started slowly in her life of crime but would eventually build an empire of numbers banks, gambling, credit scams, drugs, and whore houses. She was so good at spending money as she was making it, and her lavish ways made a lot of newspaper headlines across the world. She blew money on expensive clothes and trips, and was known to buy exotic cars, especially after being released from Yazoo Mississippi federal prison.

Most of her drugs came from Colombia. Kilos of cocaine were much easier to smuggle to the United States than the thousands of bales of marijuana that had to be loaded onto the mother ships or packed on planes and then illegally smuggled onshore into the Gulf Coast. Moreover, the profit margin for cocaine was much higher. The news report in October 1979 put the cost of a pound of cocaine in South America at $27,000, about $35,000 a pound ($80 a gram) wholesale in the United States and nearly $290,000 ($640 a gram) retail.

Several of the Colombia criminal entrepreneurs who began entering the cocaine trade became members of the Daniels Cartel, the most powerful drug trafficking organization to emerge in Colombia.

The Daniels Cartel was named after a family that lived in Blytheville Arkansas. The Daniels Cartel godfather was known as "Tubb." They came from the lower class hood and clawed their way to riches using intimidation and violence. She put a handgun to her best friend's head and blew her brains out. She was living a dream of hood wealth.

Gigi turned her head to Diamond. "Death before dishonor is dead. It's legalized slavery now, bitch. One nigga or bitch get popped by the feds, they tell on sixty other niggas, most of them don't even know. The judge told me in the courtroom, if I didn't cooperate he was going to hide my black ass for life. That old ass white woman did that when all-white jury convicted a bitch on nine homicides and drugs charges where they never found any bodies."

"How did you beat the case?"

"My cousin Justice got me a lawyer in their circle. I won it on appeal in the 8th Circuit."

"It figures," Diamond laughed.

"They got factories in all the federal prisons," Gigi continued. "The judges have investments in the federal prison system like some kind of livestock. They give niggas these big ass numbers, fines that they know they can't pay or time they can do without health problems. Most of them go working in the kitchen or Unicor just to make a few dollars. Some dudes work all day in the kitchen and make $21.00

dollars a month to the point he steals items just to make a living outside the kitchen with stolen kitchen food."

"Damn, bitch, why won't the community or the people that can do something about it, do something?" Diamond asked innocently.

"A bitch don't know. People on some ice out time and all the churches are exploiting so much money. Shit, in prison, 95% percent of snitches claim to be religious or in a gang."

"Get the fuck outta here," Diamond said she opened the door to let some fresh air in.

"One thing a bitch learns in federal prison, religion and the so-called Holy Bible or anything else are the biggest brainwashing tools on the earth. Fuck, was we heathens in Africa before they brought us over on ships here and gave us a religion that don't belong to us? Teaching that bullshit about you gotta die to go to heaven when the streets is paved with gold. If that was true, then white people would be lined up killing each other just to get there. Instead, they line up killing us niggas, sending us to mythical heaven, while they enjoy themselves right here on earth." Diamond licked her lips like she wanted to mention something. "A white man's heaven is a nigga's hell."

"Baby girl, you know a bitch is a Christian around this bitch," Diamond said, disturbed.

Gigi retorted, "Bitch, you the one who asked me what prison is like."

Moments later, they dropped the duffle bags off at an old, run-down house that Gigi bought. Afterward, they decided to ride through their old hood on Lilly Street, flaunting the luxury car. They were drinking Hennessy and Coke soda. Gigi puffed on a large blunt. She had the .357 burner under her seat as they all exchanged war stories and laughed. The atmosphere was relaxed as they rode along, getting high off blunts and drunk on nostalgic memories.

The night was jumping in Thug Town, the party of the town. Gigi drove her black Audi, and Diamond was telling her where to go, and what trap spot to visit. Gigi was that bitch and just about every trap house they stopped, niggas showed love to her by giving cash. She was the bitch every nigga wanted on their team.

Niggas broke cash out of love and some did it as a way to renew their payments on protection fees. Boss bitch was back out on the street. At that time there were several Boss Bitches but which one will stand last? To some, that was mind-boggling, because many hated her, most feared her, but all respected her.

Damn it feels great to be a Boss Bitch, Gigi thought as they rode around town, bending blocks in the Audi. Shit was looking great, even by her standards. She glanced over at Diamond as she snapped her fingers, jamming to the music on the radio, going to that place where women go when they're truly relaxed, looking fine and don't even know it. She bolted straight forward in her seat and looked at Diamond's nice breasts. Her clothes concealed her nice tattoo.

As Gigi turned down Wall Street, the block that Mustafa's cuz lived on, she noticed an unmarked Honda car pulled up behind her. She had the handgun in her lap. The unmarked car was all on her ass bumper. Furtively, she passed Diamond the heat. She placed it in the hidden compartment.

"You straight?" Diamond asked from the passenger seat as they pulled into the driveway.

"Yeah, the cops are right behind a bitch. Hold that fuckin' drink down, crazy bitch."

Diamond turned around and saw Captain Snow getting out of his car. He walked up and tapped on the driver's side window to the Audi; Gigi lowered it slowly. Snow fanned the air as the scent of weed drifted from the car window into the gray haze of the streetlights.

Captain Snow did a triple take at seeing Gigi behind the wheel of such an expensive update car.

"Shit! Gigi. How in the world did you get out of prison?"

"The feds slipped, I gripped, same old bitch. You know how the game goes when you have money and know people in big places."

Captain Snow ducked his head down to get a better view into the car. He saw Diamond in the passenger's seat. She had her arm on the armrest with her hand poised under her chin. Her manicured fingernails glistened as she rubbed her chin.

One thing that Captain Snow had to admit, Daniels Family Cartel was a seasoned hustler and even a cold-blooded killer. Even the Mayor of the city was forced to respect their operation.

"What, it's your turn to beat a bitch this time?" Gigi questioned sarcastically, reminding Snow of the situation in the past.

"Listen, Gigi, why don't you let that shit go?"

"Like hell," Gigi retorted as she got out of the Audi, her height towering over the Captain.

"One day you'll find out I'm one of the good guys," he remarked as he shoved her a duffle bag. "It's going to take Uncle Tom black ass police officers to stop white police brutality."

"Yeah, and what is it going to take to stop cops from killing unarmed black people and getting away free?"

Captain Snow, lost for words, stood there and looked at her.

"Y'all have a nice day." Captain Snow walked back to his car.

"Bitch, you see that duffle bag Snow had? It probably was dope and money he stole from a drug dealer," said Diamond.

Chapter 20

Two hours later a black Cadillac limousine came to a stop beside Gigi.

"Where the fuck we at?" Ace yelled, looking out the window into the pitch-black darkness.

The window divider that separated the chauffeur from the passengers opened. A woman wearing a Chicago Cubs baseball cap, ponytail and dark shades stuck her head in the window and announced tersely, "Somebody said you were looking for this bitch!"

The red beam from the .45 handgun bounced around off the two bitches' foreheads as it ominously stabbed at the darkness until it finally settled on Diamond's forehead.

"Bitch, you goin' around town talking shit about me."

"Baby girl, I don't even know you," Gigi responded, her voice hinting at a plea.

"Aw, bitch, you know me. I'm the bitch you were looking for. You called me out, so I'm here."

Her neck snapped back like she had been slapped when she realized who was sitting across from her with a gun leveled at her head.

"Listen, woman, I ain't got nothing against nobody," Gigi said, knowing that the first real law of the streets code was to never buck a jack move.

She reached into her pocket and removed a large water pistol. "Bitch, Imma let you choose your weapon of death for both of y'all which is better than the chance you gave me."

Gigi looked at Sister Mary, narrowing her eyes at her and said, "What, you crazy or something?"

Sister Mary smirked as she calmly aimed the real gun at Gigi's shoulder and fired. The blast from the gun was deafening in the small confines of the Audi.

Gigi hollered, as well Diamond screaming for not to shoot Gigi again. "Aw fuck, aw fuck, you fucking shot a gangsta bitch!"

She grabbed her right shoulder with a face stricken with both pain and terror as she looked at the mad woman sitting across from her. The red beam from the light continued to tease her mind as it roamed across her chest and head. Diamond whimpered as she looked on with her hands in a prayer position.

Diamond looked on with fear-filled watery eyes. In an attempt to distance herself from her wounded friend, she slid her body as far away as the limited space would allow. She mumbled something to herself.

The muffled sounds of the chauffeur screaming in the trunk disturbed Sister Mary. The man in the trunk promised to be quiet. Sister Mary made a mental note to shoot a big hole in the trunk key hole before she departed.

Sister Mary was the most feared woman in the world. She had run her Cartel for many decades and killed several Cartel members in her circle. "If you wanna live, bitch gotta die," Sister Mary said, pointing the gun at Diamond. Just then Sister Mary handed Gigi the gun to shoot Diamond. "Damn, we got a major problem," Sister Mary said. The cops are headed in this direction.

"Fuck!" Sister Mary cursed under her ski-mask. She knew that if she suddenly drove off, it would surely get her pulled over, and if they started, the police would look into the car. Sister Mary got out of the car and walked right toward them while Gigi and Diamond drove off to the nearest hospital.

Chapter 21

A couple of weeks later, Junebug and Teresa landed at Memphis Airport. They traveled light with a Louis Vuitton duffle bag filled with two hundred thousand dollars in cash and another bag with five days' worth of clothes for each of them. Per Teresa's instructions, Junebug was to go outside, pull his cell phone from his bag and wave it at the first Lexus limousine that he saw. Junebug did it without hesitation. A white Cadillac limousine pulled from behind a row of waiting cars and taxi cabs.

He looked at Teresa. "That gotta be the ride."

Teresa lifted the Louis Vuitton bag and wrapped the strap across her shoulder. When she stepped off the curb, Junebug followed behind her with the other duffle bag and cell phone in his hand. At the rear passenger door of the limousine, a black female chauffeur waited and greeted them with a bright, pleasant smile. Teresa stopped, and out of respect, she stepped to the side and allowed Junebug to enter first. He got in and she got in behind him. The door closed.

Inside the limousine, a soft, elegant song played, and the words were in Spanish. Across from them, a light brown Colombian man in linen pants, sandals, and a white wife-beater shirt looked at them. He had on a pair of Gucci expensive designer shades. He slowly bobbed his head to the music, never saying a word to either of them. The limousine moved out into traffic, muscling its way onto I-55 interstate.

The Colombian continued to watch Junebug and Teresa until Teresa broke the silence.

Junebug threw his head back. "What up, bro?" His eyes fixed on the Colombian.

The Colombian still didn't part his thin lips.

The phone inside the limousine rang and the Colombian answered in Spanish. He listened to the voice on the other end. "Si, Auntie Maria," he finally said. Then he listened further. He removed his shades and sat them on the seat next to him. "Si, Auntie Maria." His facial expression changed. "One moment." His deep Spanish accent sounded very intimidating.

He politely handed Junebug the phone.

"Hello."

"You made it, I see."

"Yes, brother, I'm here."

"Introduce yourself, stay on top of everything you stand for, and remember, your word is everything. I'll contact you every day to get a full updated status."

"Okay, talk to you later." He handed the Colombian the phone and he hung it up.

Now his attitude had changed. He extended his hand out to Junebug, and he shook it. "I'm Santo, my friend."

"I'm Junebug," he said, then pointed at Teresa. "This is my best friend, Teresa, right here."

Santo let go of Junebug's hand and shook Teresa's. "Teresa," he said with a smile, revealing ivory-white teeth with oval shaped diamonds on each of them across the front. Teresa stared at his teeth in amazement.

"Damn! How much you paid for your diamond teeth?"

"A whole lot of cash and selling drugs. You like them?"

Teresa's eyebrows hunched together and her pussy got wet in the midst of the conversation. "Hell yeah, player."

Santo flipped his wrist to check the time on his watch. No more than twenty-five minutes later, they were traveling down Beale Street. They made a left onto Third Street and proceeded over the bridge until they got to the entrance to Arkansas. They stopped at the riverfront for a minute.

From the rear of the limousine, Junebug and Teresa gazed through the tinted window at several yachts and cruise ships. The limousine finally came to a halt. The panel window that separated the rear of the limo from the front rolled down. Junebug and Teresa both turned their heads and looked at the sexy black Cuban girl, but her stare was directly on Santo.

"Are you boarding now?" she asked.

Santo nodded, gave her a smile, and she rolled the partition back up and switched off the engine. Teresa looked at Santo. "We getting on a boat?"

Santo eased his shades back on his face. "*Yacht,* my friends, far better than a boat."

The female driver opened the rear door and Santo eased around and stepped out. He inhaled the fresh air coming from the river. Horns blared from ships. When Teresa and Junebug stepped out, the girl closed the door. Santo led them to the entrance of a private yacht.

They walked through a sea of people, up a flight of stairs and across a small plank with metal hand railings. Santo was greeted by a short guy dressed as a crew member for the luxury yacht. Junebug and Teresa both stared around in amazement. They had never experienced or seen anything like this in their lives.

"Allow me to take your bags," the short guy said to Junebug and Teresa.

Teresa looked at him, and then her eyes shifted to Santo. Santo bowed his head, giving her permission. They entered the yacht's interior through a pair of automatic sliding doors. The inside was laced with exotic woods, including handcrafted maple burl and eucalyptus. There were marble floors and thick carpet. Santo led them down a hallway, bypassing a wine cellar and an exercise gym with a glass wall. Finally, they stopped in front of a shiny brass elevator. He pressed a button and the doors opened.

"Man, I didn't know a yacht had elevators." Teresa said as they entered the elevator.

No one responded. The door closed, and Santo pressed a button that had the letters *MT* on it. They went to the next floor and the doors opened. When they stepped off the elevator, they saw beautiful women everywhere. Some were naked and some in string bikinis. A tanned Chinese chick stopped in front of them with a white tray filled with custom cigars. Her hair hung down to her waist, her breasts were exposed, and she wore only a pair of black and pink thongs and matching heels.

Santo removed one of the cigars, Teresa followed by grabbing one, and Junebug did the same. They continued to follow Santo. Women were stopping her to kiss her hand and each of her cheeks. Santo stopped and said something in Spanish, and two young thick females appeared. Both were very sexy; one of them was Cuban and the other was a Brazilian cutie.

Santo pushed the door open into one of the guest cabins. It had wall-to-wall thick carpet. Two queen-sized beds and an octagon-shaped Jacuzzi sat in the middle of the floor facing a glass wall with a view of the Mississippi river.

"You two stay here," he told Junebug and Teresa. "Beautiful girls, champagne, cigars…" He waved his hands in the air.

Junebug and Teresa moved into the room and the girls stayed with them. Teresa licked her lips for some freak action. Santo turned and left for a minute and closed the door behind him. The Cuban and Brazilian girls began to undress them both. The young Brazilian girl led Teresa to one of the beds. She laid back and rested on her elbows. She went straight for her pussy and slipped it in her mouth, working her tongue and lips like a professional headhunter. Junebug looked down at her, and began toying with her rose-red nipples, as his mouth got really wet. Teresa closed her eyes as she took the fire head that was given to her. *Have you ever had some fire ass head that make your body shake?* she thought.

With a half-smile, Teresa winked at Junebug as the Brazilian girl pushed her closer to the edge with her skill. Teresa's pussy started making all kinds of sounds before busting into the Brazilian chick's mouth. Junebug was smiling and his dick was hard. He wanted to fuck the chick but Teresa wasn't going to let that to occur. This was something that Junebug never saw coming, and he was left wondering what the fuck was going on. Teresa got up and put her clothes on and exited the room. Junebug walked behind her smiling, but mad deep down inside. He wanted some of that Brazilian pussy bad.

***

Diamond drove Gigi to the hospital full speed, passing every car in sight, as Gigi continued to scream in pain, holding her shoulder with a T-shirt. They arrived at the hospital and exited the car. They went inside to the front desk and spoke with the clerk.

"May I help you?" the woman at the desk asked.

"Yes, you can."

"Oh my God," the woman hollered and requested for help, opening the door for them to come toward the back where the doctor was. Gigi was rushed inside a room. The doctor and nurses attended to her right away, trying to remove the bullet from her shoulder. About twenty minutes later, the bullet was successfully removed and more work was done to make sure she was okay. The medicine that was giving to her put her to sleep. She was excited to have the bullet removed once she woke up.

"Thank you, Doc," Diamond told him. Before leaving the hospital she hugged the woman at the front desk and tears rolled down her face at the same time. Diamond couldn't believe that someone would shoot Gigi just like that and think they will get away. The police at the hospital tried several times to find out who shot her, but she wouldn't say anything. She understood the street code: *Don't snitch and don't steal from nobody.* You will get killed and probably put your family's life in danger forever. That was the kind of Ruthless Boss Bad Bitches she had encountered.

Chapter 22

Con climbed into the shower and closed his eyes, allowing the water to massage his body. This past year of Con's life had been hectic. Niggas robbing his trap houses on the eastside of town, niggas coming up short, and he was trying to maintain different relationships with several beautiful women. He had to make his presence known more in the streets and buckle down on his hustle squad.

Ever since Con had been fucking with Angel, shit had been different. His other girl, Karen, always had some shit to cry about, and she no longer cooked and cleaned like she used to before he got released from federal prison. It was different with Angel. It felt like she was put on earth for him. She was so caring and understanding. Con could have a long day at the trap, and she'd meet up with him just to chill and later get dicked down.

After finishing his shower, he walked into his bedroom, where Angel was laying across the bed wearing a little t-shirt and thong. His dick bricked up just from looking at her body. Today, she was free because nigga had to fly back home to handle some business. She felt like she was about to cheat on her man, even though she was with Con first. Con was stressed and in need of a nut real fast. Angel's cycle was kicking in, so she'd been cramping, which meant Con wouldn't be able to get his dick wet with her today. It had been a while since the last time Angel and Con had sex anyway, so he was like, fuck it.

He climbed into bed with her and spread her legs using his knees. Then, he lifted her shirt over her head and kissed her on the lips. She held onto the back her of his neck and kissed him back, wet mouth. Con broke the kiss. He trailed kisses down her soft body. Finally, he ripped her thong and placed three fingers inside her.

Angel rocked her thick hips slightly, as Con picked up the pace. Then he put his head between her legs and dipped his long tongue in and out.

"Stop, Con, you know I don't like that. I'm wet now, so just put the dick inside me," Angel whined.

Con chuckled inwardly because Angel hated receiving head and giving head, while Karen loved having his head buried between her thighs and slobbing on his dick. Releasing a sigh, Con removed his hands and hovered over her. Con slid inside her and lifted one of her legs in the crook of his strong arm, so he could get a good rhythm. Angel's pussy felt good as hell and wet as fuck.

"Damn, Angel, your shit wet as hell, baby. Let me find out you missed this huge dick in your guts," he groaned as he picked up the pace.

"Yes, nigga, I missed this pipe. I'm about to cum, baby," she announced loud.

Con kept the same speed until she was shaking and cumming all on his dick. He flipped her over and shoved his dick in from the back, pushing Con deep inside her so he could go deeper inside her pussy.

"Ouch, ouch, ouch! Pull out some that dick, baby. You're in too deep," Angel complained out loud.

Con moaned and groaned like a pitbull and pulled out his dick some. Angel had just pissed him off by fucking up his rhythm of hard strokes. He was tempted to just pull out and go beat his dick off in the shower, because he was no longer in the mood. He closed his eyes and pictured Karen throwing her ass back on him while getting fucked, and just like that, he nutted inside Angel ten minutes later.

Rolling over on his back, he threw his arm over his eyes as he thought about his dilemma. Angel had some good wet pussy, but it was a waste of time and boring. She only liked to have sex in doggy style or missionary, and she couldn't take much dick. She also thought oral sex was nasty, so he might as well give up on trying to convince her that it wasn't. Con knew he was her first, so he tried to be patient and teach her little steps, but it had been many years. If she hadn't learned by now to please a nigga she would never learn.

Karen and Con's other bitches, on the other hand, were the total opposite. He felt like he was going backwards every time fucking with Angel. Having sex with her was like a 9 to 5 job. When Con was fucking with Karen, though, he just wanted to live in her pussy for days at a time. She allowed him to bang her whenever, wherever, and however he wanted with no complaints. If he looked like he was stressed, she'd slob on his knob without him even having to ask.

Con pulled Angel into his arms and laid with her for about thirty minutes strong until she nodded off to sleep. Careful not to wake her up, he climbed out of bed, grabbed a pair of boxers and his clothes, and then headed to the bathroom to freshen up his dick. He had a minor headache, so he looked in the medicine cabinet to find some Tylenol when he saw Angel's birth control pills on the shelf.

He was surprised when he opened the cabinet to find birth control pills. When he saw the bottle was still full, he was instantly mad. He searched through the cabinet even more to see if there was another bottle somewhere. He exited the bathroom and went into the room to wake Angel up.

"Yeah!"

"Angel, what the hell is this?" he yelled with the bottle in his hand.

"Huh? It's my birth control pills." She rubbed her eyes.

"No bullshit. Why the bottle full?"

"Well, it's been a couple years since we lost our baby." Angel thought now was a great time to get pregnant.

"Nah," he read her mind, "right now isn't a good time," Con said quickly.

"Con, I don't see what the big deal is. We live together, and the right time will never come. It's not like we can't afford it. You're not planning to leave the game anytime soon. I'm bored and tired of being at home alone. At least if we have a baby together, I'll have something to do and someone to keep me company all the time."

Con looked at her ass like she was crazy. He felt like she was trying to trap him and ruin his whole life even more. If he was to get her pregnant, there was no way he could break things up with her while she was pregnant. He didn't want to raise a child in a broken home. He grew up without a father and also his brother, Justice, so he always said that if he had kids, he would never put them or their mother through what he went through growing up.

His mother and father were married for about eleven years. She had him, in her hands, and everything was good with them, but when she got pregnant with Justice, he was gone with the wind before her third doctor appointment. Leaving her to struggle with a three-and-a-half-year-old while pregnant. He never attempted to reach out or pay child support. As far as he knew, his ass died in federal prison.

"I'm sorry. Angel, we can't do this anymore." He sighed as he sat on the edge of the bed.

"You can't do what, Con? I know you are not breaking up with me because I been missing for a minute. We don't have to have kids now. I can start back taking my birth control pills to make you happy."

"It's not just that, Angel. Everything is moving too fast for a nigga. I wasn't ready for us to be involved with each other anymore. I'm not ready for a baby now, we're not on the same page right now. To be honest we want different things in life."

"Really, dude, so after everything a bitch put up with from you, you're blaming me and calling it quits? I will leave my nigga for you and stay here with you. A bitch robbed several banks just to make sure that we will be straight."

"Wow! I'm not blaming you, Angel. I'm not faulting you for wanting more than what I'm ready to give. You're a good woman, and deserve everything you want."

"I love you, Con. There's no other person I want to be with. I can be patient with you. I'll do whatever you want. I know I'm not satisfying you in bed like that bitch Karen. You want me to suck your big dick? I can handle that. You want me to get freakier when we have sex? I can do that too. I'm willing to do whatever to keep you around. Please, just don't leave a bitch," she begged as she cried into tears.

"This isn't about love, Angel. You know a nigga will always love you. We were business partners before anything. I just need some time and space to myself to get my thoughts together. I'm going to stay at my old crib for a few days, so you can really think about what I said. We will sit down and talk later." Con pulled her close to him. Con couldn't bring himself to break her heart even more. He was afraid to love again after being heartbroken in the past. He stayed with her for two long hours until she calmed down, then he grabbed some clothes that he would need at his other crib.

Twenty minutes later, he went to the trap spot and picked up his homie, Thug, then they hit the streets to do awesome drop-offs and pick-ups. After that, they chopped it up at the trap and counted money for several hours.

"What's up with you, bro? You look like you got a lot on your mind," Thug said.

"Yeah," Con said. "I broke things off with Angel temporarily so I could focus on my shit out here in the streets."

"Man, I don't blame you, you should have ended things with Angel a long time ago. I looked at the way you're with Karen. I can tell you're not happy anymore."

"Nawl, that bitch tried to kill me in the past. You're right. That's why I ended things. I hate lying to people, and being with Angel seems wrong. I'm doing her more harm than good by stringing her along all this time."

Con told Thug everything that had been going on with him and Angel's so-called relationship, all the way to her trying to get pregnant without telling him anything. It felt good talking to Thug and getting everything off his chest.

Con stayed at the trap for an hour before leaving. He was on the way home to his crib where Angel was staying at for the moment.

Chapter 23

The following morning, Con woke up to one of the best feelings in the world. For a minute, he thought he was dreaming like a baby until he opened his eyes and saw Angel's head bob up and down as she sucked and slurped on his dick. She had her hand wrapped around it, stroking as she went up and down. She looked him directly in the eyes as she twirled her tongue around the tip of his hard dick, causing him to moan like a bitch. Con tried his best to hold that shit in, but he couldn't.

"Fuck, baby, suck that dick just like that, baby," he groaned. Con leaned his head back to break eye contact because the way she was looking in his eyes while giving him fire head had him ready to bust a nut already. It was one of the most beautiful sights he'd ever seen.

"Look at me or I'm going to stop," she threatened. He couldn't believe she was using his own tactics.

Con did as he was told because he didn't want this feeling to stop. He wanted to see if she was going to actually let him cum in her mouth or not. If she let him cum in her mouth, she would have his heart; maybe have his ass ready to go buy her a fat ass diamond.

Angel continued to stroke his dick before she took his balls into her mouth. She had a nigga toes curling and eyes rolling in the back of his head. Con thought Karen gave good head, but she ain't have shit on Angel. Con grabbed the back of Angel's head and she picked up the pace in the race, causing him to moan even louder. "I'm about to bust," he warned Angel.

When she didn't move, he shot cum down her throat. She made sure to catch every single drop of his seed. She continued to suck him dry. It felt like she was trying to suck his soul out of his dick. Con guessed this was payback from last night when he wouldn't stop eating her pussy. Con couldn't take it anymore, so he pulled her up to him and kissed her, not caring that she had just swallowed his babies down her throat.

Con sat up against the headboard and Angel eased down on his dick, causing a moan to escape both of their mouths. Her pussy was wet as hell, just from sucking dick. Shit like that made Con's dick even harder because that meant she enjoyed pleasing him just as much as he enjoyed pleasing her.

"Shit, Con, this dick feels so good," she whimpered as she moved up and down on his dick. He held onto her neck and applied a little bit of pressure, and Angel crazy ass started smiling as her eyes rolled back and her mouth went in an O shape. She held onto his shoulders and picked up the pace. Her little freaky ass was enjoying every bit of this. Con knew she was a freak the first time he laid eyes on her, and she had the nerve to act like she didn't want to give a nigga the time of day.

"Oh fuck," he moaned as she turned around and did a split on his dick. Con grabbed a handful of her thick ass cheeks as she twerked on him. It was fatter than what it was when Con first met her, and Con was loving the view.

"Con, I'm cumming, baby," she called out before squirting all over his dick. That was another thing he loved about her. It didn't take much for him to make her cum and she was a squirter, so that meant her pussy was juicy as fuck.

He allowed Angel to catch her breath, then he climbed out of bed and pulled her to the edge of it. He threw both of her legs over his shoulder and plunged into her. He watched his dick as it went in and out of her. It was coated in her cum, and he only had a couple more strokes in him before he was ready to cum.

"I'm about to nut, baby. Where you want me to release this nut?" he groaned.

"Wherever you want, daddy," she purred

"Open up," he ordered as he pulled out of her.

Angel sat up on her elbows and held her mouth wide open. Con released his nut on her breasts and in her mouth. She smiled at him as she rubbed his seeds around her nipples. The sight of it was making his dick hard again. Con pulled up from the bed and went into the bathroom to finish what they'd started in the shower. Con would have gone another round after they showered, but Con was going to give her a break because at this point, she could barely stand.

"Uhm, you tore a bitch underwear and I can't walk in those high heels right now."

Con laughed as he walked over to the bag that he brought with him last night. He grabbed a panty and bra set from it along with a Gucci jumpsuit and Air Force Ones sneakers shoes. He handed it to her, and she got dressed while Con got dressed in a pair of black Amiri jeans and a long-sleeve white fitted shirt with a pair of black Chanel sneakers.

Once they finished getting ready, they put their clothes and shoes from yesterday in a bag, then left the hotel and headed to breakfast. As soon as they got in the car to go home, Angel was out like a light. She was knocked out during the entire drive. When they made it to the house, Con gently shook her awake, smiling boastfully.

**

A week later

Con and Karen left the club, and they couldn't get back to the house fast enough. Their hands were all over each other. Luckily, they were in the back row alone so no one could see what they were doing unless they were being nosey. Had they drove on their own, Con would have pulled over and broke her off in the parking lot just to get that first nut off. She had made him horny ever since she did a sexy little dance for him. She just didn't know how bad Con wanted to lift her skirt up and fuck her right then and there. The only reason Con didn't do it was because Con hadn't had sex with her in two months, so he wanted their first time back to be right. Now, any other time, Con didn't give a fuck. If she pulled some shit like that and she had on a little ass skirt, he would've pulled out his dick and give her the business.

When they arrived at Karen's house, everyone was out back on the patio drinking. The cook had left sandwiches, fruits, and chicken wings for when they made it back. He grabbed a tray and put three champagne flutes on it, a bowl of ice, strawberries, and a plate of food for them to share. He already had a bottle of Moët upstairs at Karen's mini bar.

Con went upstairs and grabbed the bottle of Moët, then headed toward Karen's room. He walked inside the door and closed it behind him. Con placed the tray on the table in the room. He stripped out of all his clothes and laid them on the pile next to hers before walking into the bathroom. He walked around to her shower area and she was already in there. He climbed in there with her after getting the rest of his clothes off. He stood in front since she was almost done. She grabbed a loofah and lathered it with soap before washing his back with it.

"Turn around, baby," she cooed.

Con did as she said, and she started cleaning his chest. Reaching to his dick, she started lathering and stroking it slowly, causing him to close his eyes. He couldn't take it anymore; he needed to bury himself inside her. He looked deeply in her eyes before covering her lips with his. Their tongues tangled and she fought for dominance but Con won.

Con lifted her by the waist and she instinctively wrapped her legs around him. He put her back up against the wall and slowly pushed his dick inside her pussy. He was not worried about Angel at the moment, because he had Karen's sexy ass.

"Shittt," Con moaned, as her pussy wrapped around his large dick like a baseball glove. Karen's shit was dripping wet, and Karen already knew a nigga wasn't going to last long. Moving in and out of her at a steady pace felt so damn good.

"Fuck, that feels good as hell," Karen moaned in one of his ears as she bit down on the earlobe.

Con started bouncing her up and down on his dick faster and faster. Her moans and screams were echoing throughout the bathroom, and it was music to his ears. Con bit down on her shoulder and Karen tightened around his dick. She continued to do that and had him ready to nut.

"Fuck, Karen, I'm about to nut, baby. Cum with me," he groaned as he bit down on her shoulder a little harder to muffle the scream that damn near came out of his mouth. She continued clenching her pussy, causing both of them to cum together. Con's dick was jumping. Con was ready for more, but he wanted to finish in the bathroom. All the time in the back of Con's head was to kill this bitch for what she done to him and his family.

Con let Karen down gently and they finished their shower together. They dried off and he carried her back into the bedroom. He gently laid her down on the bed and moisturized her body with some baby oil. She was glistening from head to toe by the time Con was done.

They drank some of the Moët and fed each other strawberries with no words exchanged. Her lust-filled eyes stayed locked on his, like she was imagining the things she wanted to do to him, but he didn't trust this bitch.

"Tell me what's on your mind, babe. I'm at your disposal," Con told her.

"I want to ride your face with this pussy until I cum all over your goatee and mouth," Karen purred in his ear.

Con swallowed the whole strawberry that was in his mouth and washed it down with the last of his Moët, then laid back on the bed. Karen wasted no time sitting on his face. She immediately started moaning as his tongue entered her folds. She held onto the headboard and wound her hips in a circular motion. He was slurping, licking, and sucking all on her shirt. Her sweet nectar was taking Con into overdrive. He had forgotten about Angel at his crib. This was a time he just wanted to go to the club and have a nice time. He never thought it would turn out like this.

Karen picked up the pace and he could tell she was close to cumming. She was squirming and moving all over the place. He put a tight grip on her and made her take the tongue lashing he was giving her.

"Fuck, I'm cumming!" she cried out as she squirted all over his face. Con had to turn his head some because it felt like she was trying to drown a nigga in her pussy. Her juices were sliding out of his mouth, down to his goatee, and all his chest.

Karen climbed off Con's face and straddled his chest backward, as she gripped his dick in her small hands. She spit on his dick, then licked the precum before placing it in her wet mouth. *That's what the fuck I'm talking about. I don't even have to ask her to give me some head like I have to ask Angel sexy ass,* Con thought.

"Damn, baby," Con growled as she started doing her thing. There was no need for him to move an inch because he knew exactly what Karen was doing. All he saw was her nice ass in his face. She started bobbing up and down on his dick like a pole in a strip club. Con reached out with his hand across her pussy to make sure it was wet. He used his long index finger and slid it inside of her ass, causing her to hum on his dick like she was in church. He started shaking as he nutted in her wet mouth. Con removed his finger from her asshole, as she turned around and slid down on his dick. He leaned up some and pulled her left breast into his mouth, as she bounced up and down on his dick. She only lasted about eight minutes the most until she was cumming again. Con flipped Karen over on her back side and slid inside of her gently. He leaned over and placed a kiss gently on the lips and continued to stroke her slowly. "Karen, I missed the shit out of you. I missed you being mine and our special friendship. I love you so fucking much that it hurt sometimes." Con continued to give her deep strokes nice and slow, making sure he hit her spot every time.

"Ohhh, Con, I missed you too, baby," she moaned out loud.

Con continued whispering how much he loved and missed this bitch, all of his future plans for them, until she started cumming all over his dick. Tears were falling from Karen's eyes, as he continued to pound and pound her brains out. Every time one dropped, he kissed the tears away. They made love for another thirty minutes until he was nutting all in her stomach.

"Get up, Karen, let's go shower before you fall asleep," Con smiled at her.

"Con, you don't have to worry about me falling asleep. You better just hope you have enough energy to keep up with a bitch tonight."

"Damn, a nigga was trying to give you a break. I can go all night," he told her seriously.

Karen had the kind of pussy that made Con want to live in it for life. Con could make love to her for breakfast, lunch, and dinner. Her pussy was *that* good. The last time Con fucked all night was the first time they made love. The most Angel and other bitches was doing in the bedroom with sex was not that great and didn't last a long period of time.

Karen and Con went into the bathroom and took a quick shower. When they were done, they went back into the bedroom and started making love all over again. Karen wasn't bullshitting when she mentioned about fucking all night long. They took a couple of breaks from fucking between times, but her little ass was wearing him out. They were making up for lost moments.

"I'm just happy that nobody's here to see me *killing* this pussy, because I will be in prison for life," Con joked.

It wasn't until the sun started coming out four hours later that Karen decided to tap out from fucking.

Chapter 24

After sitting in the house all night, Angel decided to grab her car keys and ride around looking for Con. During the drive her phone started ringing. She looked at her cell phone and saw it was Con calling.

"Hello."

There was silence in the background, then Angel started hearing loud moaning sounds. Angel knew she wasn't tripping, so she turned up the volume on her cell phone. She heard someone talking in the background. *This nigga really got me fucked up!*

She went by the trap house first and Con's car wasn't there. She was silent on the phone, and Con had forgotten to hang the phone up at the same time. She drove to Karen's apartment and saw Con's car outside. She pulled into the parking lot and exited the car full speed. She knocked on the door like the police. One of the guys inside the apartment opened the front door without saying a word.

"Hey, Angel, what are you doing here?" another young boy asked.

"I'm here to see Con."

"We haven't seen him in a minute."

"Okay," she made her way all the way inside the apartment and saw nobody. She walked outside the apartment into another apartment down the hallway. She stopped and knocked on the apartment door, but nobody answered, so she turned the knob and it wasn't locked; so she walked in. Tears instantly filled her eyes when she saw a bitch on top of Con, riding his dick.

"What the hell is this?" she yelled as she yanked Karen off the top of him. Con looked like he wanted to crawl into a hole while Karen had a smirk on her face.

"Baby, I can explain," Con said, jumping up and putting on his clothes.

"How could you do this to me?" Angel cried.

"I'm sorry, Angel, but it is what it is." Karen started putting on her clothes and walking out the bedroom.

Angel was too stunned to even chase after Karen. "Out of all the bitches in the world, Con, you cheat on me with Karen, the one that tried to hurt you once before. Maybe her pussy and head is driving you crazy. It's sho' not her looks."

"Angel, I messed up, honey, I swear it wasn't planned out like this. I came here this morning to do some maintenance work on the apartment and she was laying in here naked. I stayed at the trap house with Thug and the other guys last night after leaving the club. I told her to put on some clothes, but she wouldn't listen. She crawled between my legs and started massaging my manhood, and I gave in like a fool."

"Fuck you and that bitch." Angel walked outside and got inside her car and pulled off. She was going about 70 mph and didn't realize the light had turned red when she hurriedly turned, and before she could complete the turn, a truck came flying toward her. She slammed on the brakes, but she wasn't fast enough. The truck hit the passenger side of her car, causing her to lose control and spin out, running into a parked car. Her head hit the steering wheel and after that everything went black.

Lock Down Publications and Ca$h Presents
Assisted Publishing Packages

BASIC PACKAGE	UPGRADED PACKAGE
$499	$800
Editing	Typing
Cover Design	Editing
Formatting	Cover Design
	Formatting
ADVANCE PACKAGE	**LDP SUPREME PACKAGE**
$1,200	$1,500
Typing	Typing
Editing	Editing
Cover Design	Cover Design
Formatting	Formatting
Copyright registration	Copyright registration
Proofreading	Proofreading
Upload book to Amazon	Set up Amazon account
	Upload book to Amazon
	Advertise on LDP, Amazon and Facebook Page

***Other services available upon request.
Additional charges may apply

Lock Down Publications
P.O. Box 944
Stockbridge, GA 30281-9998
Phone: 470 303-9761

Submission Guideline

Submit the first three chapters of your completed manuscript to ldpsubmissions@gmail.com. In the subject line add **Your Book's Title**. The manuscript must be in a Word Doc file and sent as an attachment. Document should be in Times New Roman, double spaced, and in size 12 font. Also, provide your synopsis and full contact information. If sending multiple submissions, they must each be in a separate email.

Have a story but no way to send it electronically? You can still submit to LDP/Ca$h Presents. Send in the first three chapters, written or typed, of your completed manuscript to:

LDP: Submissions Dept
P.O. Box 944
Stockbridge, GA 30281-9998

DO NOT send original manuscript. Must be a duplicate.
Provide your synopsis and a cover letter containing your full contact information.

Thanks for considering LDP and Ca$h Presents.

NEW RELEASES

BLOODLINE OF A SAVAGE 1&2
THESE VICIOUS STREETS 1&2
RELENTLESS GOON
RELENTLESS GOON 2
BY PRINCE A. TAUHID

THE BUTTERFLY MAFIA 1-3
BY FUMIYA PAYNE

A THUG'S STREET PRINCESS 1&2
BY MEESHA

CITY OF SMOKE 2
BY MOLOTTI

STEPPERS 1,2&3
THE REAL BADDIES OF CHI-RAQ
BY KING RIO

THE LANE 1&2
BY KEN-KEN SPENCE

THUG OF SPADES 1&2
LOVE IN THE TRENCHES 2
CORNER BOYS
BY COREY ROBINSON

TIL DEATH 3
BY ARYANNA

THE BIRTH OF A GANGSTER 4
BY DELMONT PLAYER

PRODUCT OF THE STREETS 1&2
BY DEMOND "MONEY" ANDERSON

NO TIME FOR ERROR
BY KEESE

MONEY HUNGRY DEMONS
BY TRANAY ADAMS

Coming Soon from Lock Down Publications/Ca$h Presents

IF YOU CROSS ME ONCE 6
ANGEL V
By Anthony Fields

IMMA DIE BOUT MINE 5
By Aryanna

A THUGS STREET PRINCESS 3
By Meesha

PRODUCT OF THE STREETS 3
By Demond Money Anderson

CORNER BOYS 2
By Corey Robinson

THE MURDER QUEENS 6&7
By Michael Gallon

CITY OF SMOKE 3
By Molotti

CONFESSIONS OF A DOPE BOY
By Nicholas Lock

THA TAKEOVER
By Keith Chandler

BETRAYAL OF A G 2
By Ray Vinci

CRIME BOSS
By Playa Ray

Available Now

RESTRAINING ORDER 1 & 2
By **CA$H & Coffee**

LOVE KNOWS NO BOUNDARIES 1-3
By **Coffee**

RAISED AS A GOON I, II, III & IV
BRED BY THE SLUMS I, II, III
BLAST FOR ME I & II
ROTTEN TO THE CORE I II III
A BRONX TALE I, II, III
DUFFLE BAG CARTEL I II III IV V VI
HEARTLESS GOON I II III IV V
A SAVAGE DOPEBOY I II
DRUG LORDS I II III
CUTTHROAT MAFIA I II
KING OF THE TRENCHES
By **Ghost**

LAY IT DOWN I & II
LAST OF A DYING BREED I II
BLOOD STAINS OF A SHOTTA I & II III
By **Jamaica**

LOYAL TO THE GAME I II III
LIFE OF SIN I, II III
By **TJ & Jelissa**

IF LOVING HIM IS WRONG…I & II
LOVE ME EVEN WHEN IT HURTS I II III
By **Jelissa**

PUSH IT TO THE LIMIT
By **Bre' Hayes**

BLOODY COMMAS I & II
SKI MASK CARTEL I, II & III
KING OF NEW YORK I II, III IV V
RISE TO POWER I II III
COKE KINGS I II III IV V
BORN HEARTLESS I II III IV
KING OF THE TRAP I II
By **T.J. Edwards**

WHEN THE STREETS CLAP BACK I & II III
THE HEART OF A SAVAGE I II III IV
MONEY MAFIA I II
LOYAL TO THE SOIL I II III
By **Jibril Williams**

A DISTINGUISHED THUG STOLE MY HEART I II & III
LOVE SHOULDN'T HURT I II III IV
RENEGADE BOYS 1-4
PAID IN KARMA 1-3
SAVAGE STORMS 1-3
AN UNFORESEEN LOVE 1-3
BABY, I'M WINTERTIME COLD 1-3
A THUG'S STREET PRINCESS 1&2
By **Meesha**

A GANGSTER'S CODE 1-3
A GANGSTER'S SYN 1-3
THE SAVAGE LIFE 1-3
CHAINED TO THE STREETS 1-3
BLOOD ON THE MONEY 1-3
A GANGSTA'S PAIN 1-3
BEAUTIFUL LIES AND UGLY TRUTHS
CHURCH IN THESE STREETS
By **J-Blunt**

CUM FOR ME 1-8
An LDP Erotica Collaboration

BLOOD OF A BOSS 1-5
SHADOWS OF THE GAME
TRAP BASTARD
By **Askari**

THE STREETS BLEED MURDER 1-3
THE HEART OF A GANGSTA 1-3
By **Jerry Jackson**

WHEN A GOOD GIRL GOES BAD
By **Adrienne**

THE COST OF LOYALTY 1-3
By **Kweli**

BRIDE OF A HUSTLA 1-3
THE FETTI GIRLS 1-3
CORRUPTED BY A GANGSTA 1-4
BLINDED BY HIS LOVE
THE PRICE YOU PAY FOR LOVE 1-3
DOPE GIRL MAGIC 1-3
By **Destiny Skai**

A KINGPIN'S AMBITION
A KINGPIN'S AMBITION II
I MURDER FOR THE DOUGH
By **Ambitious**

TRUE SAVAGE 1-7
DOPE BOY MAGIC 1-3
MIDNIGHT CARTEL 1-3
CITY OF KINGZ 1&2
NIGHTMARE ON SILENT AVE
THE PLUG OF LIL MEXICO 1&2
CLASSIC CITY
By **Chris Green**

A GANGSTER'S REVENGE 1-4
THE BOSS MAN'S DAUGHTERS 1-5
A SAVAGE LOVE 1&2
BAE BELONGS TO ME 1&2
A HUSTLER'S DECEIT 1-3
WHAT BAD BITCHES DO 1-3
SOUL OF A MONSTER 1-3
KILL ZONE
A DOPE BOY'S QUEEN 1-3
TIL DEATH 1-3
IMMA DIE BOUT MINE 1-4
By **Aryanna**

A DOPEBOY'S PRAYER
By **Eddie "Wolf" Lee**

THE KING CARTEL 1-3
By **Frank Gresham**

THESE NIGGAS AIN'T LOYAL 1-3
By **Nikki Tee**

GANGSTA SHYT 1-3
By **CATO**

THE ULTIMATE BETRAYAL
By **Phoenix**

BOSS'N UP 1-3
By **Royal Nicole**

I LOVE YOU TO DEATH
By **Destiny J**

I RIDE FOR MY HITTA
I STILL RIDE FOR MY HITTA
By **Misty Holt**

LOVE & CHASIN' PAPER
By **Qay Crockett**

TO DIE IN VAIN
SINS OF A HUSTLA
By **ASAD**

BROOKLYN HUSTLAZ
By **Boogsy Morina**

BROOKLYN ON LOCK 1 & 2
By **Sonovia**

GANGSTA CITY
By **Teddy Duke**

A DRUG KING AND HIS DIAMOND 1-3
A DOPEMAN'S RICHES
HER MAN, MINE'S TOO 1&2
CASH MONEY HO'S
THE WIFEY I USED TO BE 1&2
PRETTY GIRLS DO NASTY THINGS
By **Nicole Goosby**

LIPSTICK KILLAH 1-3
CRIME OF PASSION 1-3
FRIEND OR FOE 1-3
By **Mimi**

TRAPHOUSE KING 1-3
KINGPIN KILLAZ 1-3
STREET KINGS 1&2
PAID IN BLOOD 1&2
CARTEL KILLAZ 1-3
DOPE GODS 1&2
By **Hood Rich**

THE STREETS ARE CALLING
By **Duquie Wilson**

STEADY MOBBN' 1-3
THE STREETS STAINED MY SOUL 1-3
By **Marcellus Allen**

WHO SHOT YA 1-3
SON OF A DOPE FIEND 1-4
HEAVEN GOT A GHETTO 1&2
SKI MASK MONEY 1&2
By **Renta**

GORILLAZ IN THE BAY 1-4
TEARS OF A GANGSTA 1/&2
3X KRAZY 1&2
STRAIGHT BEAST MODE 1&2
By **DE'KARI**

TRIGGADALE 1-3
MURDA WAS THE CASE 1-3
By **Elijah R. Freeman**

SLAUGHTER GANG 1-3
RUTHLESS HEART 1-3
By **Willie Slaughter**

GOD BLESS THE TRAPPERS 1-3
THESE SCANDALOUS STREETS 1-3
FEAR MY GANGSTA 1-5
THESE STREETS DON'T LOVE NOBODY 1-2
BURY ME A G 1-5
A GANGSTA'S EMPIRE 1-4
THE DOPEMAN'S BODYGAURD 1&2
THE REALEST KILLAZ 1-3
THE LAST OF THE OGS 1-3
By **Tranay Adams**

MARRIED TO A BOSS 1-3
By **Destiny Skai & Chris Green**

KINGZ OF THE GAME 1-7
CRIME BOSS 1-3
By **Playa Ray**

FUK SHYT
By **Blakk Diamond**

DON'T F#CK WITH MY HEART 1&2
By **Linnea**

ADDICTED TO THE DRAMA 1-3
IN THE ARM OF HIS BOSS
By **Jamila**

LOYALTY AIN'T PROMISED 1&2
By **Keith Williams**

YAYO 1-4
A SHOOTER'S AMBITION 1&2
BRED IN THE GAME
By **S. Allen**

TRAP GOD 1-3
RICH $AVAGE 1-3
MONEY IN THE GRAVE 1-3
CARTEL MONEY
By **Martell Troublesome Bolden**

FOREVER GANGSTA 1&2
GLOCKS ON SATIN SHEETS 1&2
By **Adrian Dulan**

TOE TAGZ 1-4
LEVELS TO THIS SHYT 1&2
IT'S JUST ME AND YOU
By **Ah'Million**

KINGPIN DREAMS 1-3
RAN OFF ON DA PLUG
By **Paper Boi Rari**

THE STREETS MADE ME 1-3
By **Larry D. Wright**

CONFESSIONS OF A GANGSTA 1-4
CONFESSIONS OF A JACKBOY 1-3
CONFESSIONS OF A HITMAN
By **Nicholas Lock**

I'M NOTHING WITHOUT HIS LOVE
SINS OF A THUG
TO THE THUG I LOVED BEFORE
A GANGSTA SAVED XMAS
IN A HUSTLER I TRUST
By **Monet Dragun**

QUIET MONEY 1-3
THUG LIFE 1-3
EXTENDED CLIP 1&2
A GANGSTA'S PARADISE
By **Trai'Quan**

CAUGHT UP IN THE LIFE 1-3
THE STREETS NEVER LET GO 1-3
By **Robert Baptiste**

NEW TO THE GAME 1-3
MONEY, MURDER & MEMORIES 1-3
By **Malik D. Rice**

CREAM 2-3
THE STREETS WILL TALK
By **Yolanda Moore**

THE STREETS WILL NEVER CLOSE 1-3
By **K'ajji**

LIFE OF A SAVAGE 1-4
A GANGSTA'S QUR'AN 1-4
MURDA SEASON 1-3
GANGLAND CARTEL 1-3
CHI'RAQ GANGSTAS 1-4
KILLERS ON ELM STREET 1-3
JACK BOYZ N DA BRONX 1-3
A DOPEBOY'S DREAM 1-3
JACK BOYS VS DOPE BOYS 1-3
COKE GIRLZ
COKE BOYS
SOSA GANG 1&2
BRONX SAVAGES
BODYMORE KINGPINS
BLOOD OF A GOON
By **Romell Tukes**

CONCRETE KILLA 1-3
VICIOUS LOYALTY 1-3
By **Kingpen**

THE ULTIMATE SACRIFICE 1-6
KHADIFI
IF YOU CROSS ME ONCE 1-3
ANGEL 1-4
IN THE BLINK OF AN EYE
By **Anthony Fields**

THE LIFE OF A HOOD STAR
By **Ca$h & Rashia Wilson**

NIGHTMARES OF A HUSTLA 1-3
BLOOD AND GAMES 1&2
By **King Dream**

GHOST MOB
By **Stilloan Robinson**

HARD AND RUTHLESS 1&2
MOB TOWN 251
THE BILLIONAIRE BENTLEYS 1-3
REAL G'S MOVE IN SILENCE
By **Von Diesel**

MOB TIES 1-7
SOUL OF A HUSTLER, HEART OF A KILLER 1-3
GORILLAZ IN THE TRENCHES
By **SayNoMore**

BODYMORE MURDERLAND 1-3
THE BIRTH OF A GANGSTER 1-4
By **Delmont Player**

FOR THE LOVE OF A BOSS 1&2
By **C. D. Blue**

KILLA KOUNTY 1-5
By **Khufu**

MOBBED UP 1-4
THE BRICK MAN 1-5
THE COCAINE PRINCESS 1-10
STEPPERS 1-3
SUPER GREMLIN 1-4
By **King Rio**

MONEY GAME 1&2
By **Smoove Dolla**

A GANGSTA'S KARMA 1-4
By **FLAME**

KING OF THE TRENCHES 1-3
By **GHOST & TRANAY ADAMS**

QUEEN OF THE ZOO 1&2
By **Black Migo**

GRIMEY WAYS 1-3
BETRAYAL OF A G
By **Ray Vinci**

XMAS WITH AN ATL SHOOTER
By **Ca$h & Destiny Skai**

KING KILLA 1&2
By **Vincent "Vitto" Holloway**

BETRAYAL OF A THUG 1&2
By **Fre$h**

THE MURDER QUEENS 1-5
By **Michael Gallon**

FOR THE LOVE OF BLOOD 1-4
By **Jamel Mitchell**

HOOD CONSIGLIERE 1&2
NO TIME FOR ERROR
By **Keese**

PROTÉGÉ OF A LEGEND 1&2
LOVE IN THE TRENCHES 1&2
By **Corey Robinson**

THE PLUG'S RUTHLESS DAUGHTER
By **Tony Daniels**

BORN IN THE GRAVE 1-3
CRIME PAYS
By **Self Made Tay**

MOAN IN MY MOUTH
By **XTASY**

TORN BETWEEN A GANGSTER AND A GENTLEMAN
By **J-BLUNT & Miss Kim**

LOYALTY IS EVERYTHING 1-3
CITY OF SMOKE 1&2
By **Molotti**

HERE TODAY GONE TOMORROW 1&2
By **Fly Rock**

WOMEN LIE MEN LIE 1-4
FIFTY SHADES OF SNOW 1-3
STACK BEFORE YOU SPLURGE
GIRLS FALL LIKE DOMINOES
NAÏVE TO THE STREETS
By **ROY MILLIGAN**

PILLOW PRINCESS
By **S. Hawkins**

THE BUTTERFLY MAFIA 1-3
SALUTE MY SAVAGERY 1&2
By **Fumiya Payne**

THE LANE 1&2
By Ken-Ken Spence

THE PUSSY TRAP 1-5
By **Nene Capri**

DIRTY DNA
By **Blaque**

SANCTIFIED AND HORNY
by **XTASY**

BOOKS BY LDP'S CEO, CA$H

TRUST IN NO MAN
TRUST IN NO MAN 2
TRUST IN NO MAN 3
BONDED BY BLOOD
SHORTY GOT A THUG
THUGS CRY
THUGS CRY 2
THUGS CRY 3
TRUST NO BITCH
TRUST NO BITCH 2
TRUST NO BITCH 3
TIL MY CASKET DROPS
RESTRAINING ORDER
RESTRAINING ORDER 2
IN LOVE WITH A CONVICT
LIFE OF A HOOD STAR
XMAS WITH AN ATL SHOOTER